GOING VIRAL
_____

NICK WYCKOFF

Nick Wyckoff
Copyright 2015
ALL RIGHTS RESERVED

Ebook ISBN: 978-0-9914448-4-7
Paperback ISBN: 978-0-9914448-3-0

For information about permission to reproduce portions of this book or information about other books in this series, visit:
http://www.watermountprojects.com/

https://www.facebook.com/KalisunInitiative/

Cover art by Andon Monk

Other books in the KaliSun Initiative Series:
The KaliSun Initiative
The KaliSun Initiative: The Price of Progress

INTRODUCTION

The KaliSun Initiative is a science fiction series starting in the near future and spanning decades. It's a mixture of short stories and novels that explore the KaliSun Initiative's efforts to colonize space against the backdrop of a cold war between the United States and China, industrial espionage, secret research programs, and the absolute danger of space. The challenges associated with this push for the stars lay bare the mortal peril to those involved, forcing them to answer a dark question. What cost are they willing to pay to shape their destiny?

CHAPTER ONE

Martin Knudsen stood silently in the back recesses of his company's secure datacenter. His two bodyguards were working in a floor vault nearby. A tall, thin man of Scandinavian descent in his late 50s, he wore the relaxed "tieless business casual" fashion popular with CEOs of the day, and carried with him the air of the elite businessmen of decades past. Under his calm façade was all the anxiety of a man taking a calculated risk.

Knudsen watched intently as Elliot, his bodyguard and aide, placed the last of the sequentially numbered hard drives on the desk. The other bodyguard, Micah, emerged from the concealed locker in the floor, carefully closed the lid, and pushed a sculpture over it.

Elliot dusted off his hands before running a meaty fist through his sparse hair. He opened a large waterproof and shock-resistant briefcase, gesturing to the second bodyguard to help him. "Micah, let's get these loaded into the case."

They carefully inserted the drives into cutouts in the foam interior, one row for drives marked yellow and one for drives marked green.

"You're sure we have everything?" Knudsen asked uneasily, looking down at his watch with a frown.

"Yes, the green ones are the jamming research, the yellow is the radiation detection research," Elliot replied patiently. "I've checked twice, it's all there. Classification markings have been removed, as well as any reference to Knudsen Advanced Research."

"You checked the metadata in the files? The markings on the inserted graphics?"

"Yes Mr. Knudsen. It's been sanitized. If anyone ever finds this data, there will be no links back to you. We will have complete deniability. I've also arranged for a cyber penetration into one of our supplier's data systems. It won't be successful, but if the government starts snooping around, it'll draw their attention over there," Elliot said.

Knudsen relaxed into a smile. "I hope you were careful, I'd hate for a bit of misdirection to draw their attention."

"Don't worry sir, I hired some kids to do it. It'll be clumsy and it's unlikely to get past the first layer of security," Micah said with satisfaction. "No connection to us."

Knudsen nodded thoughtfully. He ran his fingers across the tops of the hard drives and his wedding band made a soft clicking sound on each of them.

"I wonder at the cost. So close to my end and I am gambling my life's work for more time." His hand rested on a single drive. "Do you suppose she would approve, Elliot?"

"Your wife?"

"Yes."

"You're not doing it for money or power. You are doing it for your child and her future children. She won't have to see sickness take the last of her family. Your wife would understand. She was never a flag-waving patriot anyway, even before the war."

"True. You know, she never understood why I changed the focus of the company from studying that leaking nuclear reactor to working on defense projects to fight the Chinese. I tried to explain to her that sometimes we don't get to choose where our paths take us, that the world shapes the lives of those who live in it. But I don't think she agreed."

"I never thought we'd lose to the Chinese," Micah said. "Their economy and military have never been as strong as ours."

"We didn't lose," Elliot said sternly. "We were forced to stop fighting. We never surrendered and, while we lost Portland and most of the Pacific Fleet, they lost millions of people too. I don't expect that they'll recover anytime soon, not after we popped Three Gorges."

Micah shrugged and looked to Knudsen, who was still eyeing the hard drives.

"I discretely asked my contacts in the Senate about what the KaliSun Initiative is up to, trying to figure out why they want this information. It took a lot of digging before I found somebody I had enough leverage with to tell me that the KSI is being funded under the table to develop technology in violation of the PACRIM Treaty. Our military, and some parts of the government, never accepted the ceasefire. They are using the KSI to develop a roadmap to the next evolution of the military... for when the war goes hot again, I guess," Knudsen said soberly.

"If that's true, then trading information with the KSI is actually patriotic," Elliot said thoughtfully. "Maybe our piece of the puzzle will prevent the next war from even happening."

Knudsen slowly closed the case, latching it and tugging on the lid to make sure it was secure before angling the handle toward Elliot.

"I doubt the next war will be on Earth. Most of the KSI's infrastructure is at the moon base they built before the last war. Whatever they want this info for, whatever the government wants them to use it for, I doubt it's to prevent a war," Knudsen said, gesturing toward the door. "If I had to hazard a guess, it's intended to help win the next war."

Micah moved to open the door, checking the hallway before motioning Elliot to move out. They exited the server room and walked quickly through the building. It was the Saturday of a three-day weekend. The employees were all gone, and the janitors were done for the day. They passed row after row of empty cubicles, some filled with plants and family photographs, others bare apart from the minimal metal furniture and office supplies.

Martin occasionally glanced into a cubicle as they passed, recognizing a smiling face in a photo or name on a wall. His company was relatively small, and many of the employees had worked for him for years. His brow furrowed as guilt racked his conscience.

They reached the garage and Micah slid behind the wheel of Knudsen's custom executive sedan. Elliot put the case in the trunk and locked it, then climbed into the back seat with Martin. The car drove silently through the underground garage, its electric engine barely making a noise as the darkness of the garage gave way to a bright southern California afternoon. Micah calmly guided the car through the heavy traffic, silent and alert for threats.

"Having second thoughts?" Elliot asked, studying Knudsen's face solemnly.

"A few."

"Because it's the KSI?"

"Because I'm trading away the hard work of my employees, my life's work—much of which was paid for by the government, yes—but also my investors... Trading it away for my own selfish benefit."

Elliot smiled, shrugging his large body in an exaggerated, devil-may-care way. "Well, you did say if it worked out you'd see if they could treat me, too. So technically, you're trading it away for both of us." Elliot pulled at his aging face with one hand and ran the other through what was left of his hair.

Knudsen cracked a half smile and looked over at him. "It's just that... with the KSI, there's no telling how they'll use what we give them."

"I think we know they won't use it responsibly. That hasn't been their path so far. Look at the way they built the Moon Based Training Center; if the IRS ever audited that mess they'd never figure out where the money came from. The good news is, I'm almost positive they are the best on the planet at keeping secrets, which makes the deal you're making a lot safer. Look at some of the stunts they've pulled. Almost nobody expected what they did out by Saturn and they've had non-stop visitors at their moon base. Somebody should've noticed something."

"You mean suddenly building a base out of nowhere?"

"Yeah, exactly. One day they're doing research on the moon and bringing up space tourists. The next day, boom, there are spaceships nobody's ever seen before hovering around their space station. I still remember the panic on social media, thinking the nuke war between us and the Chinese had attracted some kind of aliens, as if that would ever happen."

"As much as Stokes makes me nervous, I do have to give him credit. He's exceptionally talented at obscuring his objectives. They built the MBTC and everyone turned their attention upward to see what they're doing up there, meanwhile the research they're doing down here is truly groundbreaking. Any idiot with money could get to the Moon, but what they're doing here... that takes vision."

"Well, if getting to the Moon was that easy, I think people would have settled it long ago," Elliot said. "But I get your point. That new base they're building out around Saturn, it's insane. Again, it's got everyone looking up instead of inward at what they're up to. I'd bet nobody really knows what Stokes's plan is, maybe not even Stokes. It's all plots within plots with that guy."

"That's what makes me nervous. Does any deal with them last through the next milestone on their schedule? It wouldn't take much for them to inject me with something lethal during the procedure," Knudsen said thoughtfully, drumming his fingers on the armrest.

"If you're worried, I'll call their man and cancel it," Elliot said.

"No. No, I've made my choice. Now it's a game of trust. Trust in their science. Trust in their word. Worst case, if I die, my daughter will get a hefty life insurance policy. How's that for a contingency plan?"

Elliot shook his head, unimpressed, but he remained silent as the sedan entered the Knudsen estate. Micah parked the car at the back of the house where it couldn't be seen and got out, checking to make sure none of the house staff were around. He gave a satisfied nod to Elliot who grabbed the case from the trunk and they headed inside.

Knudsen's daughter Helen spied them from her perch in the kitchen. She put her candied apricot down and raced after them, catching up with her father as he approached the stairs.

"Dad!" she called out excitedly. "You remember, my birthday party is starting soon! *Please* don't work through it, it's so important to me that you be there the whole time."

"I promise, I won't miss it. For too long I've prioritized work over family. Look what it cost me—your childhood, your mother's health. Soon, very soon, things will change. I promise you that I will stop working so much and we will make up for lost time. There will be time... I will make sure there's time."

He leaned in and kissed her forehead softly, brushing a stray strand of blonde hair away and turning to walk up the stairs.

"Just remember Dad, you are getting old," Helen teased, hands on her hips.

He paused, turning back toward her. "Old in spirit, but I am willing to wager that this body will last quite a while longer. Have no fear. Now hurry off and get ready for your party."

He watched her turn, a tender smile on his face, before he climbed the stairs to his office where Elliot and Micah waited with the case.

"Holly, please play some music from your favorite album," Martin said as he entered the room.

"Of course, Martin," the house computer responded in a perfect rendering of his wife's voice. Soft harp music began playing—a recording of his late wife's last concert.

Martin walked to his desk and stood looking soberly at the case.

"It'll be worth it," Elliot said.

"Maybe. It's very important to me that my daughter knows our family history, that she understands the legacy she will be responsible for. She is all I have left. I need time to have an impact in her life."

He reached past the case and picked up a framed photo of Helen and himself in Costa Rica, cradling it in his hands for a long moment before handing it to Elliot.

"Put it in the safe. Put anything connected to my personal life into the safe. These people like to hunt for leverage and information. Let's not give them anything we don't have to."

"Do you want me to station Micah outside the door during the procedure?"

"No. We need to appear confident in the deal. Remember, they are just as guilty of intellectual property theft as we are, so it's important we convey trust. If they wanted to stir up any trouble, they probably wouldn't send the doctor here, or Lavoy for that matter. As I understand it, they have more effective ways of taking care of problems. No, we've taken all the precautions we can."

"They should be here in an hour," Elliot said, checking the screen on his phone. "What do you still need to do?"

"Examine my life choices," Knudsen said dryly as he sat down heavily in his chair.

Elliot nodded and proceeded to pace the room, collecting personal objects and photos—anything that the KSI might not already know about—and putting them in the wall safe.

CHAPTER TWO

Traffic leading to the Knudsen estate was heavier than usual. The discretely armored sedan wound its way through the wealthy California suburb, and the deeper it drove into the enclave, the more ridiculous the houses became, each trying to outdo the neighbors with more expansive architecture, lawn sculptures, security systems and landscaping.

"If they spent half as much energy on developing their businesses as they do on this crap, we'd never survive," the driver said over his shoulder to the elderly German in the back seat.

"Steve, we live in a world where simply being the best isn't good enough. You need flash; you need recognition. Without all that attention, their lives feel hollow, without substance. It's sad, but ultimately to our benefit."

Steve Lavoy snorted, but held his tongue as they approached the Knudsen compound. The front entrance was covered in a mass of balloons, and two off-duty cops were checking identification. He slid the sedan in behind a half-million dollar supercar and inched forward as each car was allowed in.

"Figures... Hang on Doctor Kapple, there's going to be a bit of noise," he said as the car turned into the driveway, its skid plate scraping along the decorative paving stones in a shower of sparks. "We're supposed to park away from the photographers, so give me a minute to get over there."

"No rush. If there is one thing this deal has working for it, it's time."

Lavoy maneuvered around the line of cars and onto a narrow road that led to the back of the eight-acre compound. He parked behind a large sculpted shrub on the edge of the pristine lawn and waited. Within seconds, an enormous, balding man stepped out of a side door and approached the car. Lavoy and Kapple exited the car and followed the bodyguard into the house.

"Nice to see so much green given the drought the last few years," Lavoy commented.

The bodyguard gave a disdainful snort and led them past a dozen rooms each decorated in the style of a different historically significant northern European kingdom. Before leading them up a set of ornate stairs lined with family portraits to the second floor.

They entered a cavernous room at the back of the house where a gaunt man stood in repose, staring pensively at the opposite wall. Steve set a briefcase on the desk and his backpack on the ground, and then looked expectantly at Knudsen.

"When I was younger, the thought of month-long business trips never fazed me." Knudsen reached out and touched a framed set of triathlon medals on the wall. "Train for a triathlon? No problem. Hell, I even won a few. But now I find time clawing at me. A month away is a month away from my daughter. A triathlon might kill me. But you—you arrive with the gilded cup of immortality. I question if this is opportunity, or some Faustian deal, best left undone."

"I assure you, this is opportunity—" Lavoy began, but Knudsen held up his hand.

"Have no fear, Mr. Lavoy, I'm too far down this path to turn back now. You'll get your data, despite my reservations." He paused, tapping his hands on the case on the desk. "My integrity for longevity. A heavy price to pay."

Lavoy gestured out the window at the finely dressed crowd gathering on the lawn to celebrate Helen Knudsen's eighteenth birthday. "More life with your daughter and, who knows, her future children. More time to make an impact on the world, to change the world for the better."

"I'm not sure that media circus out there changes anything for the better, but it's what she wanted. Kids these days feel they aren't special if they aren't famous." Knudsen nodded slightly before continuing. "But we should get this over with. On the hard drives you will find a complete archive of Knudsen Advanced Research's RF jamming prototypes, and copies of the research we've done for the Department of Energy on remote radiation detection. This should more than jumpstart your program. Almost thirty years of research and product development on the promise that your treatment works."

"I assure you it works, Mr. Knudsen. Steve was one of the first test subjects. He had inoperable pancreatic cancer. Not only did this treatment reverse the growth of his tumor, it has arrested his aging processes by almost seventy percent. He was an early subject, and we've improved the treatment significantly since then," Doctor Kapple said.

Lavoy affirmed this. "My treatment was almost five years ago. If you follow the guidelines we give you, you will have many years ahead of you. In my case, the cancer may return some day. My treatment was imperfect and will probably need to be repeated at a later date. But right now, I feel great and I've already lived four more years than I should have."

Micah leaned into the room to announce that the party was starting in an hour and ducked out again. Lavoy and Kapple exchanged a glance. Lavoy smiled and pointed at the door.

"Maybe we should lock that."

Martin signaled Elliot, who left the room and locked the door behind him. "Nobody will bother us with him out there. Let's get started."

"Some information before we begin," Doctor Kapple said sternly. "First, this treatment is transported into your body via a virus. We used a rare virus for which we have an effective treatment, weakened it, and inserted a set of genes into it. The virus will remain in your body permanently after the treatment cycle has finished. The gene set is specifically tailored to your DNA. It works by rejuvenating portions of your genome that have aged by using your own DNA to reset the clock, so to speak. As the cells age, the virus continues to reset the clock, slowing the aging process dramatically. That's why we needed to conduct extensive testing beforehand, and why we needed the bone marrow sample. It is very important that you understand and agree to the next statement. If you have sex with somebody with a DNA profile that is substantially different from your own, you could kill them. The virus will be transmitted through fluid transfer, infect them, and try to change their cellular structure. You have indicated that at your age, you are not interested in sex and that this will not be a problem. Additionally, you will never be able to donate blood again, even to your daughter. Before we begin, you must confirm that you fully understand and agree to refrain from exposing third parties to this treatment."

"Yes I understand, no sex with people from other races."

"No. Even if you have sex with a white person of similar ancestry, you most likely will have dissimilar DNA. After you get this treatment, the only people you will be able to have sex with are other treated people. Forever. Is that clear?"

"So I could have sex with somebody who was treated, but from a different race? That doesn't seem right."

"If they have been treated with their own tailored virus, it will safeguard them against infection. However, you should know so far we've only treated men. So your options are limited."

"That seems poorly planned," Knudsen laughed.

"We haven't figured out yet if there are problems with pregnancy after treatment, whether the virus gets carried over to the baby and what the consequences are of a baby's exposure to its mother's DNA alterations. We are currently running tests on animals, but for now, it is only men."

"Makes sense. Okay, I got it. Send anyone I want to have sex with to you for proper testing to make sure we're compatible."

"Uh..." Lavoy looked to Doctor Kapple for guidance.

"Yes, that'll work. Now, for the actual procedure. It won't take long. I'm going to give you an injection, and in about three days you will run a fever. We'll send a nurse over to check on you, but after two days the fever should subside and you will begin down the path to feeling young again. Any questions?"

Without a word, Knudsen rolled up his sleeve, exposing his arm for Doctor Kapple, who hesitated with an awkward smile. "We'll need to check the data on those drives first to make sure it's legitimate."

With a quiet snort, Knudsen pushed the case toward Lavoy, who unpacked the drives and hooked them to his laptop. Minutes ticked by as the computer scanned through the volumes of data. Satisfied, he gave Kapple a nod.

"Here we go, a small prick and then on to your extended future," Doctor Kapple said as he gently inserted the needle into Knudsen's upper arm.

Knudsen pulled his sleeve down and watched the security feed as the two men left the compound. They blended in with the steady stream of VIPs coming and going, the only difference being the barely detectable security features of their car.

"They're gone, and not a moment too soon. Party starts in ten minutes," Elliot said from the window.

"It was necessary. If the wrong people found out what I paid for my treatment, longer life would be a penalty not a benefit. Helen's party was good cover. The effects of the virus won't hit for a few days, and when they do I can claim that somebody coughed on my drink."

"I'm not saying it wasn't smart, I'm just saying we need to get down there before she makes her entrance," Elliot replied.

"Of course, let's go."

They wound their way through the house and out into the throng of partygoers. A mariachi band worked their way through the crowd and the dozen or so small bars scattered across the lawn had people milling around them. Close to five hundred guests, shoulder-to-shoulder, were mingling, networking, ass-kissing... and trampling his beautiful lawn.

"When I was young, a keg and a pickup truck were all you needed for a great party. Now look at this mess. Somebody asked if we were going to have any animals. Bunch of adults apparently need a petting zoo," Knudsen said as he made his way through the crowd toward the stage and microphone.

His progress was slowed by greetings from business acquaintances and local officials, each taking a moment to pose for pictures or thank him for inviting them. Just before he reached the stage the mayor cornered him for a photo, stumbling against him slightly, clutching a drink and suggesting rather loudly that Knudsen could host a fundraiser at his house.

Knudsen smiled for the picture, promising discretely that

he'd have Elliot contact the mayor's office to set something up and apologizing for needing to get on stage.

He strode out into the spotlight, tapping the mic a few times before holding his hands up for quiet. The crowd gradually quieted and turned their attention to the stage.

"I want to thank all of you for coming today. As you know, today is my daughter Helen's eighteenth birthday, a special day that marks her transition from high school into the next phase in her life. It's an exciting time for me, too. It's been just over six years since Holly—love of my life and Helen's mother—passed away, and in that time Helen and I have become incredibly close. She's a great kid—good grades, positive attitude, everything a father could hope for and more. So it is with great pleasure that I introduce the latest adult Knudsen—Helen!"

His slender daughter, hair in a pile of blonde curls and wearing a spectacular sequined party dress, bounced out from the back of the stage, pausing to give him a kiss on the cheek before taking the mic.

She let out a big cowgirl whoop and held the mic up for the crowd to respond, the younger sector of the crowd enthusiastically screaming in reply.

"Thanks, Dad! As you all know, I hate giving big speeches, but I wanted everyone to understand how much I love you and appreciate you coming out for my big day. So without any further chitchat, let's get this party started! Allow me to introduce my favorite band, Back Alley Coyotes!"

A curtain dropped at the rear of the stage and a motorized platform slid forward, the band already starting to play a country ballad. The lead singer sidled up to Helen and gave her a big hug before inviting her to sing with him.

Martin smiled with genuine happiness, watching as Helen's friends rushed forward at the sight of the band. He'd made it a handful of steps from the stage before the media cornered him.

"So Mr. Knudsen, how does it feel to see your daughter turn eighteen? It looks like you spared no expense. The Coyotes alone make this a party for the ages!"

"Well you know, your daughter only turns eighteen once, so I wanted to make it special for her. Besides, if you have the money, why not spend it?"

"It was so gracious of you to allow the media access to the party. And what a lovely estate you have. So much green!"

"We do our best. Obviously, we have to be careful with our water usage, but we do pay the bill at the end of the month," Knudsen said with a laugh. "Last question."

"Samantha West, CelebNews. What would you say to all of the kids in the city who aren't as fortunate as your daughter? You could have used the money for them."

Knudsen's face stiffened, but his smile remained. "My company provides mentors to children at disadvantaged schools and donates money to the civic fund every year. At the end of the day, that is charity, and this is a reward for my daughter. Thank you."

He turned and walked away as Elliot spotted him and elbowed his way over. In the background, the reporter yelled out a parting question. "Reward for what?"

Knudsen ignored her and headed toward one of the bars, talking to Elliot as he went. "Let's not invite CelebNews to the next function, and keep an eye on her tonight."

"You got it."

After a brief stop at the bar, Knudsen sat down in a lounge chair under an almond tree and watched the party from afar, sipping a Macallan Scotch over a single ice cube. The reporter's question ate at him. Yes, the party was overkill. But he'd worked long and hard to earn his money, and there was no reason not to spend it on his daughter.

His gaze lingered on the reporters. If they thought the party was a big deal, imagine if they knew what he'd paid for his treatment. His brow furrowed and goose bumps rippled up his arms at the thought.

CHAPTER THREE

"Are you sure you don't want me to stay?" Helen drew her hand across her father's forehead and checked his temperature one more time. "It's not a big deal. We're just going shopping with my birthday money."

"It's fine, don't mind me. I've got an in-house nurse coming. You go have fun, enjoy yourself. I'm sure I just caught something at the party. How are you getting to the Galleria?"

"I got a ten pass card for my birthday for the new drone cabs. It's great. They pick you up and take you right where you want to go. They have their own lane on the freeway and you don't have to deal with any smelly cab drivers."

"Times have certainly changed. Well get going and don't be late getting back. I've got Ronnie making your favorite dinner tonight."

"Alright, I hope you feel better. Love you, Dad!" She said, tucking the blanket around him

Knudsen pulled his tablet out and watched his daughter on the security monitor until the drone cab pulled up. She pushed her ID and gift card into a slot in the door, and the door opened for her to climb in. With a satisfied sigh, he set the tablet down on the coffee table and reclined into a nap.

He woke with a start when he felt the blanket being pulled away. He struggled to focus for several seconds before realizing it was the nurse Dr. Kapple had promised. She was in her forties and performed her work quickly without causing him discomfort or speaking to him. She gave him some water and tucked the blanket around his shoulders again. Then she pulled out her phone and sat in the corner of the room away from the window, swiping impassively.

Knudsen checked his phone and saw it was only four in the afternoon. He drifted back into a fitful sleep.

Three hours later, shouts broke through his feverish haze and made him bolt upright. It was Elliot, yelling at the nurse to get out—and she did, calmly walking out of the room and heading down the hallway, still tapping away at her phone as she went. Elliot shook Knudsen gently to make sure he was awake.

"Martin. Martin! We have a huge problem." Knudsen blinked up at him. "Your daughter is missing."

"Wait, what?" Knudsen peered groggily around the room, dim in the last light of the setting sun.

"Helen is missing. The cab she took never showed up at the Galleria. Her friends called the house a few minutes ago to tell her that she'd missed a great shopping day; Ronnie answered and told them that Helen was supposed to be there. I just got off the phone with the cab company. They can't locate the cab that picked her. It's been removed from their network."

Knudsen struggled to get up.

"I called the police and got them looking for the cab. Then I called Corporate Security and let them know."

Knudsen shook his head for clarity. "Call Lavoy, tell him we need to speak with him right away."

"Why Lavoy?"

"His boss knows people who can get things done in a hurry." He closed his eyes and mumbled, "We'll need all the help we can get. And get that nurse back up here."

Micah escorted Lavoy through the house to Knudsen's office, pushing past police officers who were interviewing the house staff and corporate security agents who were stationed near the doors. The KSI nurse was hovering over Knudsen on the couch administering medication. A half-dozen corporate suits were in the corner talking quietly, and Elliot was speaking with a tall, dark-skinned police captain. Lavoy quickly sent a single and walked over to Knudsen.

"Good evening Martin. I take it all is well?" he said with a meaningful glance toward the police captain.

"No, all is not well, Mr. Lavoy."

"I trust Becky is seeing to your needs and the police aren't required to render further aid?"

"This is not about my fever! My daughter. My daughter is missing."

Lavoy looked genuinely taken aback. "Missing?"

"Yes, missing. She left for the mall earlier today and, according to her friends, never arrived." He gestured for Lavoy to lean in closer, his voice a carefully measured whisper. "I need to know that your people didn't take her. That you didn't snatch my daughter as leverage for some reason. I've heard how you operate when your interests are in danger."

"When we make a deal, we honor it to the end, Mr. Knudsen. We don't have any reason to need leverage with you, do we?"

"No," Knudsen hissed. "I'm sorry. I shouldn't have jumped to conclusions. I need your help, I need you to find my daughter. I know your boss knows people who can find people. I will compensate you, whatever the price. Please. Help me find her."

Lavoy stood up and stared down at Knudsen neutrally. "That captain is local police right?"

"Yes."

"Let me see what we can do. Give me an hour to arrange a meeting with the captain and one of his detectives. We may have somebody that can help resolve this."

"You will include my corporate security team as well."

"No, we will not. The fewer people that we involve, the less mess to clean up later. Right now we don't know who kidnapped Helen. I know it's not somebody from our corporation. I don't know it's not you, your assistant, the local police, or somebody else making a power play from inside your corporation. I don't know if this is because of our deal or not, and because of all those unknowns, we are going to keep this very small. That way if word gets out, we'll know who to see about it. Clear?"

"Yes. Make your call."

Lavoy turned and walked out of the room. Knudsen watched on his tablet as Lavoy moved through the building, out the front door, and into his car. The car rumbled to life, a small antenna popped out of the roof and the windows darkened.

Knudsen paced the room, his hands gripping his elbows tightly. Most of the police officers were gone, and he'd moved his corporate security team to the other end of the house, leaving just the nurse, the police captain, one of the detectives and Lavoy.

"You said an hour, it's been nearly two."

"The boss decided to get you one of our best men. He'll get here when he gets here."

The detective interjected. "In my experience, the first hours after a kidnapping are the most important. We shouldn't be sitting around waiting for your man."

"Where would you search? Who would you question? It's not like she wandered off the edge of the property or got lost hiking somewhere. She was picked up by an unmanned car and driven somewhere else. The car has vanished; she's vanished. We have one chance to get this right," Lavoy replied calmly.

"No offense Mr. Lavoy, but we are professionals; why should we expect the addition of your man to make that much of a difference? We have the resources of our entire police department at hand, including some of the best detectives in the state," Captain Jackson gestured over at the detective.

"A reasonable question," said a voice from the door. All heads turned. "I would ask you to consider a few things. One, whoever hijacked Ms. Knudsen's car likely took the liberty of penetrating your networks before doing so, so they could observe the progress of your investigation. Two, this was not a random act and won't be solved by a random investigation. Three, if your opponent has had plenty of time to study the chessboard, and you have not, the only way to restore balance to the game is to add an unexpected piece to the board. My name is Joe Lehman, Mr. Knudsen."

Joe walked quickly across the room, stopping in front of Knudsen and looking intently into his eyes. He was a large man in both presence and build, with closely cropped hair, shaven face and quiet, controlled body language. When he moved all you heard was the whisper of fabric on fabric, with barely the sound of a footstep to mark his passing.

"Thank you for coming."

They gathered around Knudsen's ornate burl slab desk; Knudsen sat flanked by the police officers on his right and the KSI advisors on his left. The young detective pulled out a small tablet and began to list off facts about the case, but Joe reached out and gently turned it off. She looked up from the dimming screen in anger, but he spoke first.

"As I said, assume whoever kidnapped Ms. Knudsen has penetrated your network. If I may, I will summarize the case."

She retorted, "You just got here Lehman, how could you possibly know the case?"

"Call me Joe. An eighteen-year-old high-school graduate attempted to go to the mall to spend a large sum of birthday money. She used a drone cab. It picked her up and never arrived at the mall. Six hours later her absence was noticed and police were informed. Shortly after that, our office was contacted. The cab is off grid. The missing person has no history of a jealous ex that might be involved." He gave her a pointed look. "You are Detective Tasha Strauss and have been with the department five years. Your boss is Captain Darryl Jackson who has held this post within the department for three months. Your office has close to twenty open murder and rape cases, and most of your detectives are overworked. You currently have no leads as to where Helen Knudsen may be—no activity on her cards or phone."

Detective Strauss steamed. Jackson closed his eyes and rubbed his temples. "That about sums it up, yes. The news media will find out about this at any moment, at which point my department is going to be hip-deep in shit."

Joe grunted and turned to Knudsen. "We have to assume that whoever took your daughter is highly competent."

"You seem to know an awful lot considering you just got here," Tasha said evenly. "We aren't even sure she was kidnapped. The cab could have malfunctioned and just driven her to the wrong place."

"I had two hours to read, and he"—he jerked his head at Lavoy—"forwarded me the details." Lavoy gave her a small, sarcastic wave.

Tasha pressed her lips together and leaned back, her eyes sliding over to the captain, but he shook his head slightly and looked back to Joe.

"I'm interested in your input, Joe."

"If you try to force this, it could have adverse consequences. Until we receive some kind of communication, either from Helen or whoever took over the cab she was in, we need to assume it was a kidnapping, and that whoever took her is watching to see how we react. We're going to react the way they expect us to in order to avoid betraying our hand. Since this is a high profile case, they will expect you to hold a press conference put your best people on it. You are going to hold that press conference, and you are going to have several of your detectives on stage with you. Detective Strauss won't be in that group. That way they will expect the team they see to be the team that investigates, and hopefully that will hold their attention. In the meantime, Detective Strauss and I will be doing our own investigating. Your main team collects, collates, and processes all the evidence; we disappear behind their façade. We don't produce any reports, we don't send any emails, we don't make any calls using police equipment."

"You want to use my officers as cover?"

"Yes. They do the grunt work, the canvassing, forensics if we get lucky. The press covers them; we work under the radar.

You know. Mr. Knudsen knows. Nobody else. Your lead detective needs to email Detective Strauss instructing her to interview the cab company. Make sure the email indicates that she is being pulled from a normal assignment to do this and that she isn't in charge; call it surge support. Then we'll go there and pull the logs, see if we can sort out how somebody took the cab."

"We? You're coming with me?"

"Yes, it would make sense for you to have a partner."

"Usually the lead detective is older than the junior detective, I'm not sure how much sense it's going to make with you following me around," Tasha said.

A smile played at the corners of his mouth but he withheld comment.

"So, the police investigate as normal and you two run open loop on the outside hoping to catch the kidnapper off guard? That's the plan? I'm sorry, this isn't exactly filling me with confidence," Knudsen said, fighting back tears.

"The plan will change as soon as they make contact. We were hoping that they'd reach out before the police press conference. 'Don't talk to the police or else' kind of thing, or some kind of ransom request. But since they haven't we just have to play our cards," Lavoy said.

"There is going to be a lot of media scrutiny on this one. We need to find her quickly. The longer this goes on, the harder it's going to be to keep the investigation in-house. We've already notified the FBI, and they're sending two agents," Jackson said to Knudsen. "They've also promised a hostage negotiator and associated team if it comes to that. In the meantime," he turned his attention to Detective Strauss and Joe, "I want you two to work together. As a *team*. Understood?"

Tasha gave an abrupt nod. Lavoy stood and shook Knudsen's hand, briefly locked eyes with the the nurse, and walked out of the room.

"From now on minimize your phone use, leave it off unless you need it. Use a burner if possible. Tonight we'll get the techs looking through all the traffic camera feeds in the city, see if we can trace the path the cab took after it left the house. Tomorrow, bright and early, we hit up the cab company and see what's going on there."

Tasha pulled her phone out and powered it down. She stood and tugged at her jacket before holding her hand out to Joe. He paused ever so slightly before taking her hand and giving it a firm shake.

CHAPTER FOUR

Detective Strauss pulled her unmarked police cruiser into the parking lot of *Zoom! Personal Valet Service* at precisely eight in the morning. The lot was nearly empty, only four cars parked under the shade of a solitary tree.

"Where are all the workers?"

"I suspect this is all the cars this place sees in a day. It's an automated cab company. A few engineers fine tuning the programming and collecting data analytics, with the rest of the support using phone apps and overseas call centers. My skim last night indicates they barely even pay taxes in the United States; most of it runs through a shell company in Ireland."

"So we have to interview engineers? This is going to be annoying," Tasha said with a disgusted sigh.

Joe shot her an amused look and got out of the car. They walked across the parking lot and had nearly reached the door when it flung open and a nervous man appeared in the doorway, tie haphazardly slung around his neck, shirt partially untucked. He ran his hands nervously through his hair and composed himself before sticking his hand out to shake theirs. Neither Tasha nor Joe made any effort to greet him.

"I assume you are the, uh, police? Come to investigate our missing cab from yesterday?"

"Yes, we'd like to question some of your technicians about what happened and look around the office."

"Uh, do you have a warrant?"

"A warrant? No, I do not have a warrant. Warrants are for people we think are guilty of a crime. We're here to understand more about how your cab system works. Should I get a warrant?"

"No, no, that won't be necessary. You can come in." The man backed up, bumping into the glass door awkwardly as he ushered them into the building. Tasha and Joe exchanged amused looks and walked inside.

"I'm Nathan Beck, I'm the manager in charge of operations and sustainment here at *Zoom!* I can help you with any questions you have," he said, trying in vain to lead them into a conference room.

"We'd prefer to talk to the technicians first, get a feel for the day-to-day operations and what they might be able to help us look for. When we're done we're going to request you support us with some data mining of your system," Joe said matter-of-factly. "Ideally you can provide us with some data so we can chase down where our missing girl may have ended up, and recover both her and your missing property as soon as possible."

"Our missing property?"

"The cab?" Tasha said, raising her eyebrows.

"Oh right, the cab. Of course," his eyes flicked between them for a second, and he continued, "Right this way, we'll go see our lead tech."

He led them down a hallway, passing empty offices and a dusty break room, before finally stopping in front of a heavy security door with an advanced biometric scanner. He inserted his badge and put his hand on the scanner, waiting for the device to finish before he grasped the handle and yanked mightily on the door. A blast of frigid air caught Tasha by surprise, causing her to take a half step back.

"Sorry, we have to keep the room cool for the servers," Nathan said as he led them past rows of servers and networking equipment.

Compared to the dusty underused portions of the building, the server room was pristine. Network cabling was neatly bundled in overhead trays, precise labels on every rack detailed what each piece of equipment did and what it connected to. The floor was marked with colored stripes indicating which zone of the city the servers were responsible for.

"This has to be the most organized server room I've seen in a while," Joe said as they walked down the corridor.

Nathan paused and gave him a strange look, then replied, slowly. "Our primary tech is a bit eccentric and can be difficult to work with, but my senior management tells me I have to use him because he is the last original architect."

"What happened to the others?" Tasha asked.

"I don't think there was good rapport in the work group. His idiosyncrasies can be really annoying. I think you'll see why."

Tasha gave a noncommittal grunt and followed Nathan around the corner to the tech's workspace. The desk was neat, everything in its place, but the walls around his cube were covered with pictures of celebrities—with their pets, on vacation, leaving a restaurant. None of the pictures appeared to be of his own family or friends. The single personal token was a picture of him and a college-aged woman standing next to the first *Zoom!* cab outside their office. A man, probably late twenties, sat with his back to them, headphones on, staring at several screens of data rapidly flowing past. In the corner of one of the screens was a broadcast from CelebNews daily. The man's hair and beard were precisely trimmed, and he wore neatly pressed clothes.

"Brian? Hey. We have visitors that need to speak with you."

The tech slowly turned around, giving his boss a sour glare before holding his hand out to Joe, ignoring Tasha. "Brian Carpenter."

"Joe." He jerked his head at Tasha. "Detective Strauss."

"Detective," he repeated, mulling that over in his head for a minute before smiling and extending his hand. She stared back balefully at him. "How can I help you?"

Joe smiled tightly and nodded toward Tasha. She took a half step toward him. "We have some questions on how your system works. Yesterday a person taking a cab from this company vanished without a trace. As we understand it, your company can't even find the vehicle that picked her up. We'd like to understand how that could have happened."

"Didn't vanish without a trace, it wasn't in the active inventory. There's a difference," he said glaring at Nathan.

"What do you mean?"

"It was in for phase maintenance due to some spotty performance. The techs were supposed to test it on the track before it was put back into the system."

"Spotty performance? These vehicles have fewer than fifty thousand miles on them according to the records you provided the police last night. What kind of performance issues was it having?" Joe pressed him.

"I don't know. Just wasn't behaving in the way it should have been." Brian's eyes nervously danced around the room before landing on the ceiling to his left. "It was not taking the most optimal routes, which of course our cars are programmed to do."

"And that was enough to take it offline? That's not a very sound business approach," Joe said with feigned disbelief.

"It *is* enough. If the system is not effective then customers will not choose it over human-operated transport. We have to be better than everyone else," Brian said with conviction.

"Who took the cab out of service?" Tasha asked.

"I did. I sent the command when I got in that morning and it drove off to the depot for testing."

"Can you access the depot log to confirm when it arrived?"

"Yeah, of course. Simple." He turned around and hammered the keyboard. The cab's recent history popped up and Brian gestured at the screen. "See, the vehicle was getting less and less effective over the last three weeks up until the other day. Here's where I sent it to the depot and you can see here it arrived at quarter to nine."

"If we could get copies of all of that data, that'd be great," Tasha said. "Does anyone else have access to the data in this lab?"

"No," Nathan jumped in. "Brian is the only authorized system admin. We are a lean services, process-focused company, so that we can provide a high quality product at the most affordable rates." There was a hint of pride in his voice.

"I am the only local with system admin access, and then we have a remote auditor that can access some of the accounting data on the server."

"I see. What can you tell us about the vehicle's activity after it left the depot?"

"The data shows it never left. For all I know it's still at the depot right now."

"Oh, well good. We have officers heading to the depot now. They should be able to locate the car and get to work on it, see if we can find any evidence of what happened to Helen," Tasha said.

"You have officers going to the depot?" Brian glanced at his phone, clearly confused, before jerking back to them. "Do they have a search warrant? Cortez is managing the depot today and he doesn't like cops."

"I'm sure they'll manage."

"Uh, sure. Well I need to get back to work now. Is there anything else I can help you with?"

"Not at the moment, but we'll stay in touch if we need anything," Joe said, shaking his head slightly at Tasha. She blinked in confusion but went along with him.

"Thanks, Brian, you've been very helpful. Nathan, if you would lead us out."

"Yes of course," Nathan said with obvious relief.

As they turned to leave, Joe glimpsed Brian reaching for his phone, unlocking the screen, and rapidly typing something in. Joe smiled and followed the other two out of the building.

Nathan shut the door behind them and spun the lock. As they walked toward the car, Tasha turned to Joe. "Mind explaining that? We had him on the ropes."

"We're not going to get anything out of him by talking. He's just making shit up. But his phone, his phone is a gold mine."

"What do you mean?"

"When we told him we had people going to the depot, he couldn't wait to get rid of us and jump on his phone. Whatever message he's about to send, we're positioned to intercept it."

"Aw shit, I don't even have a phone to call back and get a tap on his phone. We're going to miss it."

"No we won't. I'm scanning the building, if he sends anything we'll get it."

Tasha and Joe waited behind a coffee shop a block away from the cab company. Joe monitored his laptop with an agitated scowl and Tasha poked at her coffee with the disposable stirrer.

"I'm scanning the building, don't worry," she mimicked. "And here we sit, two hours later, empty handed. If I had my phone we could have called back and at least tried to get a tap on his phone."

"He'd have intercepted the call, then he'd know we're on to him."

"You're paranoid. What does that thing do anyway?"

"I set up a ghost cell receiver near the building last night. Any calls in or out will use it instead of the normal system. It still forwards their content on to its final destination, but I get to see it first."

Tasha stopped drinking her coffee and slowly looked up at him. "Those aren't authorized for use by private citizens."

"I represent a corporation, we have a corporate security division. It's not illegal."

"Since when?"

"H.R. 721, three years ago or so. There was an amendment added at the last minute to the must-pass legislation on the Department of Education funding plus up."

"Who in Congress could possibly want that?"

Joe looked at her with a cryptic smile and turned his attention back to the device, changing some settings and sending out search pulses.

"What corporation do you work for again?" Tasha asked.

"The KaliSun Initiative," Joe said.

"Those obsessed space nerds? Why in the world would you want to work for them? All they do is sit around talking about exploring the solar system and playing around on the moon. It's just a bunch of rich playboys building sand castles in space."

"Steady paycheck, get to see the world, all that." Joe's eyes narrowed at the screen.

"What?"

"He didn't call anyone or text anyone. But he did hook up to some kind of network." Joe muttered under his breath as his big hands roamed the keyboard.

Tasha tried to follow what he was doing, but when she opened her mouth to question him, he held up a hand to dissuade her. Finally, he looked up at her abruptly.

"I think we've got a problem. I'll be right back."

Without waiting for her to respond he pulled a compact satellite phone out of his backpack and left the car, walking down the street in the opposite direction from the cab company. Tasha waited till he was rounded the corner of the coffee shop, then reached a hand discretely into his bag and rifled through it.

Inside she found a strange electrical box, a small pouch with several memory sticks in it, and an assortment of knives, tools, and a lock pick set. Joe suddenly reappeared in her field of vision and she hurriedly dumped the contents back into the bag as he approached.

He climbed in wordlessly, and reached into his bag for a cable to connect the phone and the scanner. He paused for a long moment before pulling the cable out and plugging in the system. The machine beeped and whirred softly, and he disconnected the phone and put it back in his bag.

"What are you doing?"

"I just uploaded a network map for this area that includes all of the known hubs and connections. Now I'm going to overlay what I detected before and see if I'm right."

"About what?"

"That this guy is as resourceful as he appears to be," Joe said with a grim frown. He punched several keys on the computer and an animation began to play. He watched intently for a moment, then angled the screen so she could see.

"Watch. It's playing a time lapse of the available networks. Over time you see new networks added and older, obsolete networks drop off. Watch the highlighted portion of the map."

She watched for several passes as the years counted up and different colored networks populated the screen. The newer, faster networks were brighter, and old dead networks faded to grayscale.

"It looks like a slow network is in operation for twenty years or so and then it turns gray, replaced by first a yellow network and now more recently the orange one. What's your point?"

"The old network is listed as being offline, so called 'dark fiber,' right?"

"Yes, it was old and out of date. Slow speed. Once again... your point?"

"I had Steve check the two newer networks for activity from before we got to the cab company to thirty minutes after we left. There is a lot of activity on both networks, but no new connections. Additionally, those networks are in conduit. No ability to connect wirelessly."

"You're still assuming he connected with something, but we have no evidence that he did," Tasha said impatiently. "I think you've locked in on this guy based on pretty slim evidence, and we need to move on to greener pastures. I agree he was acting sketchy, but we're wasting time. Time we don't have."

"I have one more piece of evidence."

Tasha sighed and waved him on.

"I scanned for secure networks earlier and found a whole range of them in the surrounding area. My computer has been sorting through them to see which have active data being passed, or data that is heavily encrypted. I found one iManet within a two block radius of the cab company."

"You found a what?"

"An internet-based mobile ad hoc network, an older protocol to link mobile devices to a fixed gateway. What I found was a single gateway with two mobile nodes hooked into it and each other. I couldn't resolve what the first node was. The system has no identifiers and the data is heavily encrypted. But the second node was transmitting streaming video and for whatever reason, not encrypted."

"Go on."

"It's a video camera trained on a door into a building. The video is being streamed to a gateway. I overlaid the probable locations of the gateway and guess what? It's right on top of one of those gray network links from before."

"The dark fiber link?"

"Yes. I think somebody figured out how to relight the link for their own private use."

"Can you tell what's going on in the network?"

"If I can access the cable, yes. But that camera is looking right at the building and the access point to the old fiber is probably in the data crypt under the building."

"I can get the city to do some maintenance in that area to use as cover."

"No need, we know where that fiber line goes, we just find a more convenient entry point. Scan for cameras watching it and then bide our time."

Before Tasha could respond, the police radio blared to life.

"ALL UNITS RESPOND. SUSPECT VEHICLE REPORTED HEADING NORTHBOUND ON HIGHWAY 7, POSSIBLE KIDNAP VICTIM INSIDE, PROCEED WITH CAUTION."

Tasha flashed Joe an exhilarated grin and put the car into gear, hitting the gas and veering out from behind the coffee shop, tires squealing and gravel spraying.

CHAPTER FIVE

Tasha wove expertly through the traffic, catching up to the cab as it trundled up the highway. It was traveling at the government-regulated max speed for an autonomous vehicle, the windows tinted almost black and its small caution lights flashing, seemingly oblivious to the police approaching from behind. The dispatcher's voice came through again.

"CAB COMPANY INDICATES NO CONNECTIVITY TO THE ENGINE SHUTOFF, RECOMMENDS YOU BOX IT IN TO CAUSE THE SAFETY FEATURES TO SLOW IT DOWN."

They dodged a slow moving van and got a visual of the cab right before it swerved onto an exit ramp, cutting off two cars. The left car swerved in front of the right, briefly making contact before jerking back onto the highway. Plastic and glass showered the ground. Unbalanced by the impact, the right car was forced to the side of the exit ramp, where it slammed into the plastic barricades and sent sand and water shooting into the air. The driver of the other car almost maintained control, but the back tire exploded, sending it into a skid. It slammed through the guardrail and tumbled down a hill into decorative bushes, throwing branches and flowers into the air.

Tasha managed to dodge the debris and veered onto the exit ramp. She cursed as the car filled with the smell of burnt brakes.

"Well, that should be an interesting insurance claim," Joe remarked dryly.

"Shut up."

She sped up as the cab turned a distant corner into a busy park. Tasha stared in disbelief as the cab hopped the small curb and drove through the lawn, scattering pets and people in its wake.

"Delta 79 to Dispatch. Suspect vehicle has turned into Hernandez Park."

A pair of joggers, who evidently couldn't hear the electric car coming, were sideswiped into the bushes as the cab plowed deeper into the park. Joe grimly grabbed the handle next to his head and held on as Tasha tried to follow the cab without causing any more damage. She thumbed the radio toggle on her steering wheel.

"Dispatch call for EMS. Suspect vehicle just 50d pedestrians in the area. Roll ambulances."

Ahead of them, the cab took another sudden turn, flattening some bushes and blasting through a park bench before it launched off the bank into the dog recreation pond, scattering ducks in every direction.

Tasha sped up, racing to the bank and skidding to a stop in a shower of turf and mud. She leaped out of the car and ran out into the waist-deep water, using her baton to beat on the glass of the window. Joe stepped out of the car and stood on the bank watching her.

The baton slipped out of her hand and landed with a splash in the water, the darkly tinted windows scarred from her efforts but otherwise undamaged.

"The windows have been upgraded for the passenger's protection," Joe said calmly from the shore as a crowd began to gather. "There should be an emergency access lever along the top, pull it out and push it in."

"How the hell do you know?" Tasha said angrily as she felt around the top of the cab, finding the lever and savagely yanking on it.

"I read the manual, figured we might need to get into the cab at some point."

With a loud pop, the window came free and splashed into the water. Caught off guard, Tasha struggled to pull her weapon before getting it in position and panning around the interior.

"It's empty."

Joe shrugged and turned to watch as four more police cars raced up to the scene, the small crowd backing out of the way, but with their phones up and ready. Tasha sloshed out of the water and walked over to him.

"Thanks for your help." She scowled at him.

"I did help, from the shore. If the car had blown up, no sense in both witnesses dying."

She stared at him blankly for several long moments. "Paranoid," she muttered, and walked over toward the newly arrived officers.

Joe remained on the bank, discretely filming the crowd with a small lipstick camera. His gaze wandered the area, systematically scanning for anything out of place. Finally he saw it, a small camera hooked to a light pole, pointing down toward where the car had crashed. Slightly above it was a transmitter, only the size of a deck of cards. A smile tugged at the edges of his mouth.

As the tow truck pulled the cab out of the pond, water poured from the open window and around the edges of the door. The hood was dented, and the sides were scraped. Tasha glowered back at her cruiser where Joe was playing with his laptop, evidently ignoring the crime scene. Almost as soon as a crowd had started to gather, he'd retreated to the back seat without a word.

Jackson approached, looking sideways at the car as the tow truck lowered it to the grass. The sour look on his face told her all she needed to know about how the conversation was going to go.

"Detective. Nice work," he ground out. "The forensics guys tell me that pretty much any trace evidence in the car was probably flushed out when you popped the window. I don't suppose you could have checked first?"

"The windows were completely dark, I couldn't see in except for the front window and even that was pretty dark. There could have been a person lying down in the back or in the trunk. I had to check."

The captain whistled through his teeth. "And what about your assistant? Is he actually doing anything useful?"

Tasha shrugged noncommittally before relenting under her superior's stare. "He's made some interesting observations, but most of it seems like chasing shadows. In my opinion."

Jackson digested that as he looked around at the army of forensic techs swarming around the car. "Find a way to make him useful. Now that the cab has reappeared, the pressure to find Knudsen's daughter... if we don't find her and we don't fully use this guy, Knudsen will blame *us* for losing her." He faced her again. "Don't let that happen."

He searched her face intently before leaving her to talk to the detectives in charge of the scene. With a sigh, she walked back to the car and got in.

"The cab is likely a bust," she said, without looking over her shoulder.

"Not surprised," Joe said distractedly, typing on his computer. "He would have cleaned it before it went joyriding out where we could find it."

"Water washed away the trace evidence they think, may have trashed the computer and the hard drive also. The only thing left in the cab was some graffiti. He'd used a laser etching system to leave images of Helen all over the ceiling in the cab. Mostly a central image of her sitting on a throne, feet propped up on a person's back with a wad of burning money in one hand and a glass of wine in the other. The scene is surrounded by smaller images of her tied up in a chair, tied up on the floor, trapped in a box. All the images have her eyes looking toward a dark figure etched into the door panel. No facial features on that image. No finger prints or fiber anywhere else so far."

"That's more creative than I'd expect. Usually highly technical people lack that kind of artistic vision. Interesting," Joe said.

"I think we need to hit the cab company again, see if they have any data on it. They said it wasn't responding to control signals, but maybe it was sending other data back. Maintenance data or something."

"Good idea. Should let the scene detectives do it though."

Tasha turned around in her seat and pushed his laptop screen down so she could see his face. "Why? We've already got the tech on the ropes. We'll know if he's changing his story."

Joe smiled and pulled the laptop away from her grasp, spinning it around so she could see the screen. "I knew he wouldn't be able to resist."

She stared at the screen as a high definition top-down view of the crime scene played in real time. As she watched, the camera panned over to the crowd and zoomed in on individual faces, paying particular attention to people who were visibly upset at the crime scene. The camera quickly zoomed back out and panned over to watch as Captain Jackson and the two scene detectives had an animated discussion next to the cab.

"This is why I think we should avoid going back and let those two go instead. They're the lead detectives. He's expecting them. If we do, it might get him to pay attention to us. We don't want him paying attention to us, you remember."

"You can almost read their lips with the quality of the video."

"Yes, he had it on you earlier. Thankfully you didn't say anything too interesting," Joe said with a lift of his eyebrow.

Tasha flushed for a minute, then abruptly pointed at the screen. "Where is the feed coming from?"

"Camera and small transmitter on one of the light poles along the path. Interestingly, he didn't encrypt the data. Good for us, bad for him."

Tasha looked up with sudden interest. "Were you able to piggyback the signal?"

Joe answered her with a broad smile and a couple of keyboard taps. The screen shifted to display the network path.

"It connects to the same dark fiber from earlier today. As long as he's streaming, my tracer program is working. Right now I've got the active nodes mapped out on about seventy percent of the topology. If he keeps the video running we should have the entire thing mapped out in about five minutes. It's taking longer because he's using at least two dark lines and they aren't linked together in a straight line. Either he couldn't get some of the equipment to work or he created a maze."

"No chance of him figuring out you're doing it, is there?" Tasha asked uneasily.

"Always a chance. This program is designed to defeat far

more sophisticated systems than he's using, without getting caught. That being said, we probably shouldn't linger once we have it."

"Can you tell where his main system is? His house or whatever?"

"Not yet, but I've found two spots where it dead ends at a transmitter that repeats the signal. Those nodes are encrypted and require some pretty nasty authentication to access. One of them is across the street from the cab company and one is out in the middle of nowhere, east of town."

Tasha bit her lip and then reached under the seat, rummaging around for a minute before producing a faded road atlas. She looked over at his screen, humming softly as she leafed through the pages.

"This would be easier if I could just search that site on the internet, with my *phone*."

"You have to assume he's smart enough to monitor internet searches from the crowd," Joe reassured her. "He'd know we were on to him in a second."

"I think you're giving this guy too much credit. Now that the cab is here, we need to press quickly in case he moves to get rid of her."

"In my experience, it's best to assume your opponent is better than you are. I'm pretty effective," Joe said, gesturing to his laptop. "So far he's managed to hijack a supposedly secure autonomous car, kidnap a girl, relight a dark fiber, and create a crime scene on demand. I might not be giving him *enough* credit."

Before Tasha could respond, the computer made a soft trill and a popup window indicated the network had been mapped. Joe turned the screen back toward him and peered down at it intently.

"Alright, we've got it. No additional broadcast sites, but there is a data storage device showing up on the network. It looks like the data from the various other nodes go there first. Parts of that data are then sent to the transmitters and broadcast, I would assume, to our kidnapper. Let me see that map again."

Tasha handed him the map and leaned back over her seat to see the laptop screen. They compared the network map against the atlas and Joe tapped the page. Tasha took out her pen and put a dot on the side of a country road.

"Give it a radius, let's say twenty miles. That's probably beyond his range to transmit, but it doesn't hurt to be conservative on the first pass."

Tasha drew a rough circle around the dot on the map and blew out a sigh of disappointment.

"Thought we had him pinned down, but this is still a pretty large area. There could be dozens of spots for him to hide in there."

Joe grunted noncommittally as he worked out the location of the data storage site. He made a disgusted sound and looked up.

"The data storage site is nowhere near the transmitter site. I can't tell if it's his house or some random hard drive he snuck into somebody's computer without their knowledge. We're going to have to do this the hard way."

"Now you're going to tell me we can't use the car?"

Joe closed the laptop, leaned back in his seat, and looked up at the ceiling of the car. "Just drive."

"Where?"

"In case we're being watched, drive for thirty minutes and then make a stop to buy something. Don't go in the direction of the cab company or the transmitter."

Tasha turned around in her seat and started the car, shaking her head as she wound her way through the crowds of people. The evening news had begun their broadcasts, a half-dozen reporters standing side by side with the cab in the background. From the back seat, the softest snore could be heard.

CHAPTER SIX

Tasha and Joe sat in the car studying the building across the street. It was early afternoon in the middle of the week, so there was a pretty steady flow of students walking in and out of the front door, using badges to gain entry. A campus security officer manned a desk in the atrium.

"Do we know what floor it's on at least?" Tasha asked as she peered through the windshield at the eight-level engineering building.

"Not a clue. It may not even be on a floor proper, he could have hidden it away almost anywhere. All he needed was a working computer, power, and connection to the old network."

"His school records show he had classes in this building, he must have set this up back then, found the old network fiber and relit it. Any one of these students could be an accomplice or a lookout."

"Or they could all be innocent, completely unaware the machine is even in the building. Either way, if we show up on a security camera in that building or file for a warrant and he is even moderately paying attention, we tip our hand."

Tasha used a pair of binoculars to look at the security guard and sighed.

"I doubt the guard is going to be much help. Middle aged and nosy, he's checked every single person's ID as they came in. He isn't going to agree to us searching all over the building without a warrant."

Joe's phone vibrated. He answered it, powering up his laptop with his free hand. After several minutes of scanning a map of the compound he hung up the phone and shifted the laptop toward her, expanding the image on the screen.

"I think our answer is right here. Just off campus there is a small grocery store, the owner rents out an old radio mast to cell phone companies. There is an access vault in the basement to the hardline connection the tower uses. His fiber link runs through that same trunk. Been around for years."

"Was that Lavoy on the phone?"

"Yes. He checked the topology map we created earlier against the local network map and found that access point. We need to find the network, tap in and poke around."

"Won't he be able to tell we tapped in?"

"Maybe. I have some tools that will let me isolate the link in a way that he might not spot. But we won't have long before the network's efforts to reconnect to the storage system trigger a bunch of alarms."

"I thought you said there was some kind of encryption on the data server anyway?"

"On the transmitter sites and the node back to the cab company, yes. Everything inside the outer perimeter doesn't use anything beyond a login and password. He's relying on the network being isolated and encrypted at the entry point to keep it secure. I guess he didn't want to bother keeping up with all the keys for the storage device."

"So some kid could get into it from inside that building?"

"Pretty much, at least as far as Steve could tell."

Tasha took another quick look at the map and put the car in gear, easing discretely out of the parking lot. They wound their way off campus and into the parking lot behind the Off Campus Grocery. Joe stepped out of the car and walked over to the radio tower, circling around and following the cabling down into a junction with a locked access hatch. He tugged on the lock a few times to test it and then flipped it over to look at the keyhole.

"You might want to take a walk."

"What are you planning to do?"

"Poke around in the open, unlocked vault we found."

Tasha looked at the lock in his hand and slowly spun in a circle looking for any security systems, but the dingy alley was empty of anything or anyone to witness what he was up to. She turned back to him slowly, trying to keep any emotion from her voice.

"I think we should just ask the clerk to let us poke around inside the—" She sighed in resignation when she saw the lock was already on the ground next to the hatch. She turned walked through the alleyway toward the entrance to keep a lookout.

She watched the traffic pass the grocery store, hardly any cars pulling into the driveway. Most of the shoppers arrived by bike or on foot, milling around the bins of trinkets and snacks outside or hurrying in to buy food from the main grocery inside. Nobody paid any attention to Tasha. Most barely even acknowledged the single clerk selling cigarettes and alcohol and monitoring the pot vending machine, but opted for the automated checkout instead.

Twenty minutes passed, and the clerk stood up from her stool, stretched, and looked out the window at Tasha. She gave a little wave and ambled over to the pot machine, pushing in a medical card and then her debit card as her eyes scanned the options.

Tasha was still watching her when she felt somebody behind her. She spun on her heel, hand dropping toward her waist, but stopped when she saw Joe. He jerked his head at the car and walked back without waiting for her.

She started the engine and pulled out of the alley, driving aimlessly away from the school. Joe tapped at his laptop. A cord connected a hard drive to the laptop, and he was watching the screen intently. It beeped twice and Joe looked up, then gestured to a parking garage nearby.

"Care to tell me what you found?"

"Viruses. A whole bunch of viruses. I'm not sure if he was collecting them on purpose or this was the place he quarantined all the stuff that was left over on the old network. Most of these are decades old."

"Maybe he has a retro computer virus fetish."

"I've isolated all the dangerous stuff and I'm sorting through the rest of the files. There are cell phone records, what looks like multiple people's school notes, old tests, a folder of account numbers and a bunch of medical data. All of that is dated from a number of years ago, some as much as a decade. I'm guessing that was during his time at school there. The new stuff is different. Highly compressed video files that appear to be from the inside of the cabs."

"Like a spy cam or something?"

"Yes. I opened a few of them. It's a collection of people talking on their phones, several where people are having sex, and others of couples fighting. They're chronological, but from a variety of cabs and there are time gaps. I doubt this represents all of the people who have used the vehicles—it's like he watches the data coming in and stores the ones he likes or whatever."

"Are there any video clips from the day of Helen's kidnapping?"

"I've found two so far, one from early in the morning which appears to be video of the actual moment he took the cab over. It's jerking erratically and there are alarms going off in the background. The other shows her in the car. I scanned it briefly but figured we should watch it together."

He pulled a small flexible screen out of his bag and attached it to the windshield, then plugged the tablet into the screen. She leaned in and he hit play.

The vehicle pulled up near the Knudsen estate and waited. Helen Knudsen walked out and slid some cards into the side of the cab, the video display promptly displayed her identification and the rewards card number with a gift provider displayed.

Joe paused the video and leaned in, looking hard at the information the video. After a minute he leaned back and motioned Tasha forward.

"She was given this gift card by someone named S. West. Who do you think that is?" Tasha asked.

"I'll have Steve do a drag on all possible combinations of the name and cross reference the people who were at the party."

Joe started the video again and watched as Helen sat down, dropping her purse in the seat next to her and cheerfully greeting the cab.

"Greetings Ms. Knudsen, what is your destination today?" the cab purred in a gentle female voice.

"The Galleria please!

"Thank you Ms. Knudsen, the Galleria is now your destination. Expected arrival time: forty-seven minutes. Please relax and enjoy the ride."

The cab moved smoothly away from the estate, the windows darkening and doors automatically locking. Helen leaned back in the plush seating and relaxed, playing with her phone. The cab began to play soft music in the background, gradually increasing the volume until Helen looked up.

"Oh my gosh, this is the music from my party! How did you know to play that?" Helen asked, beaming.

"This cab has been programmed to provide you with an experience you will never forget."

"Yes, but how did you know I liked Back Alley Coyotes? I mean, everyone likes them, but this is like my favorite song!"

The windows tinted darker and darker, gradually blocking out the light entirely and obscuring people outside the cab from seeing in.

"I've been watching you Helen."

Her smile faded abruptly and she looked around the cab. "What do you mean?"

"I've been watching you. Your friends and your father, too. Rich, spoiled and arrogant—hardly a redeeming quality in the whole group. You haven't had to work at anything in life. Just show up and it's handed to you. Become an adult and it's a party. Normal people have to work. Normal people have to struggle and fight and grind to be successful. But you, you started out richer than I'll be in fifty years. But today, we're going change all of that. Today, you are going to learn what it means to struggle. You are going to learn what your father will do to save you. You are going to learn your true worth," the cab's voice softly explained.

"But I'm a good person. I volunteer! I spend time with needy children, I donate my old clothes, I recycle. I'm *good*!"

"You're obscene."

Joe and Tasha watched the rest of the video in silence. Helen frantically tried to dial her phone, but it wouldn't respond. She had banged on the windows, but the cab's soundproofing and tinted windows prevented anyone from noticing. She grew hysterical, great sobs wracking her body. She begged to be released and pleaded with the cab not to hurt her. But the cab was silent.

CHAPTER SEVEN

Tasha thanked the storeowner and jogged out to the car, hopping in and immediately pulling back onto the road, buckling her seat belt as she accelerated.

"Cab passed here at 4:20 heading east. Windows were dark and it was going the speed limit."

Joe marked the time down on his notepad and compared it with the map. The line he had drawn had taken eleven random turns so far, but made its way steadily east along the county roads, inching closer and closer to the transmitter location.

"He followed the roads between these two fiber lines he reactivated. I think all the turning was so he can stay close to the active nodes on his network. Whatever he did to the cab to control it, it requires him to block the satellite signal and falsify the car's navigation data. If he just jammed it, the car would revert to safe mode and drive back to the garage."

"I'm going to swallow my pride and admit you were right about the cab guy."

"We haven't caught him yet, could also be his manager. Or they could both be in on it."

"Come on, we've cracked this thing. All we need to do is find this guy's hole and kick down the door. The case is ninety percent solved!"

"In my experience, that last ten percent can make or break you. Another gas station up ahead at that intersection, let's check their cameras too."

Tasha pulled into the dilapidated lot and parked under the overhang. Large puddles of congealed oil tarnished two of the parking spaces, and what was left of the landscaping was scorched dead from the drought. They got out of the car and Tasha strode confidently into the building, holding her badge. Joe stepped around the corner toward the bathroom, taking the satellite phone out of his pocket.

He paused to make sure she wasn't following him before dialing Lavoy. Joe updated him on their progress, and Lavoy caught him up on the state of the police investigation, including a video dump from the latest message the kidnapper had released through CelebNews. Joe cut the call and headed inside.

The attendant was showing Tasha footage from the security cameras when Joe walked in. He stopped in the snack area, staring up at the TV in the corner. Tasha saw his sudden change in expression and walked out of the back office to see what was up. Her faced hardened when she saw the screen.

A visibly distressed Helen Knudsen stood in front of a dark tarp, reading from a sheet of paper in her trembling hand.

"By now you all know that I have been taken. I am young and blessed. Blessed with my good looks and... and my father's money. I have never had to work hard for anything. My father has taken care of everything. My father has his millions and his fame, but what has he done for the community?

"How has he shared this wealth? By throwing parties for

other rich people, walling off his massive estate and riding around in private jets; nothing but crumbs given to the rest of us.

"But now his only daughter, the last of his family, is missing. It's time for him to repay the people. It's time for him to understand how unfair he's been to the rest of us.

"If the sum of fifty million dollars is not used to improve this community in the next five days, I will be... I will be..." She paused as the words caught in her throat, tears streaming down her face. She swallowed hard and continued. *"I will be killed. Please pay Daddy, please he—"*

The screen went black as the feed was cut, then replaced by a speechless anchorwoman. The gas station attendant laughed bitterly.

"Serves her dad right. Living in that mansion, getting whatever he wants, whenever he wants," the man said. Tasha bristled.

"It's a stupid ransom demand," Joe said quietly. "Even if her dad has that much money he couldn't spend it in five days and nobody could prove it if he did. Whether her dad pays or not, he's going to kill that girl."

"Just another snobby rich kid. Won't make a difference," the man said as he walked back to the counter. "All these little fake celebrities are leeches on society, not worth a damn. Won't be missed neither."

"Imagine if it was your kid that got taken." Tasha said heatedly. "Imagine somebody wanting to murder your child just because you'd found a way to be successful."

Joe shot a surprised look at Tasha, but held his tongue. The gas station attendant scowled at her, then looked meaningfully at her badge and gun before sitting down on a stool, turning his head and staring off into space. Tasha took a half step forward then thought better of it, turned and stomped outside. Joe followed, and the gas station attendant called out, "Bunch of paid killers, serving the rich. That's all you cops are. We don't owe you nothing."

Joe turned and aimed a predatory smile at the man, and an audible click sounded from inside his pocket. Instantly the lights, cameras, register and TV went dark, the power slowly draining from the emergency lights as well. The attendant sat up suddenly and reached under the counter for a flashlight.

"You're half right," Joe said. "But I'm no cop."

The attendant stood silently in the dark as they pulled away, his hand clenching the flashlight, shaking slightly as the power came back on.

"I swear it showed the car turning left at the gas station back there. It turned left and never came back through." Tasha was getting frustrated.

"Well, it didn't come back through from time you saw the footage to the time his little broadcast hit the airwaves. It might have come back through later. We won't know unless we go back and take another look at the tape."

Tasha shot Joe a petulant look, but didn't reply, choosing instead to flip through several pages of the map book spread out on the hood of the car.

He continued. "We do know a few things that make this easier. The car won't go off-road, or even attempt a road that's too rough. There hasn't been another store or place where we can check footage for the last 15 miles, just a few ranches and a lot of open space. This gas station doesn't show the car passing here. Which means he should be somewhere along this stretch of highway."

"Except we're not that close to the broadcast point. We're outside your 20 mile ring by several miles."

"He might be using a different kind of radio or a satellite phone, or even a relay. Twenty miles was just a guess. But it seems unlikely the car went anywhere other than this road."

"So what do you propose? It's been almost three days since she was taken and now he's issued an ultimatum. We're running out of time. We can't just go kicking down doors."

"Well, we can assume he had somewhere to park the car. A garage or a barn or something. He's not going to just leave it sitting out in the open. He might have some communication gear around his hiding place, and since he's holding a hostage, my guess is he doesn't want close neighbors."

"Unless there are accomplices."

"Does he strike you as a team player?"

She shook her head and stared out across the brown landscape. Nothing was moving save for a buzzard circling aimlessly high over the road. The air was still and the sun baked the pavement. She started to ask Joe about heading back to the gas station when she heard his phone ring.

"I thought you said no phones?"

"Trust me, he's not getting into this one."

"Who's calling?"

Joe smiled and held the phone to his ear. He listened intently for several seconds then motioned for her map book and something to write with. He circled four addresses on the map, scribbling notes next to each one before hanging up.

"Steve says the pressure's on to find her, and he's given us four locations to check out."

"How did he figure out which locations?"

"He analyzed all of the houses on the road, and sorted them by energy use and internet connection. None of the houses on this road connect back to our suspect, but there are four that have high levels of energy consumption and internet usage."

"He has his own network to play on, why does he need an internet connection?"

"Porn, Maybe? But he can't interact with people over his closed network without risking somebody finding it, so we're looking for somebody who likes to interact on the web and probably has a lot of tech around their home. Carpenter is clearly well schooled in the car networks so we can assume he's got ways of sending data out over the internet without it tracing back to him."

"Sounds pretty thin. I don't think we'll get a warrant with that kind of probable cause."

"So we go looking for PC. If we happen to find her in the process we can act. If we play by the rules, she might die before we get to her."

"Let's just try to avoid getting wrapped up in a police brutality case with somebody unrelated to our investigation. It might not matter to you, but I have a career to think about and it can't look like I've been playing dirty. Period."

Joe shrugged and pushed the map towards her.

She hesitated and fingered the house nearest to where they were parked. "Might as well go in order, unless you have a better plan?"

Joe took the map and climbed into the car, cranking the air conditioning to max before turning the phone off and dropping it into his bag. Tasha climbed in, wiping the sweat off her forehead and tossing her baseball hat in the back seat. She put the car in gear and pulled a U-turn.

"Something else to consider. Steve told me the kidnapper sent that broadcast video to a trashy celebrity news show called CelebNews and demanded they air it. They were hesitant to do so and called the police to ask them how to proceed. Apparently they took too long to respond and the kidnapper forced his way into the feed for the news broadcast we saw at the gas station."

"How long did he wait before he hacked the network?"

"Less than thirty minutes. Steve said it took the police a bit to process what CelebNews sent them and get in touch with the detectives, who were down at the maintenance depot. Within ten minutes of the phone call, the hack occurred."

"So he's impatient," Tasha said. "All the more reason to get this done."

"I think it's more than that. CelebNews doesn't have that wide of a viewership, certainly no contacts within national media. It's a local celeb show, barely above a web series."

"True. On the other hand, they were present at Helen's birthday party. So maybe that's why Carpenter keyed in on them."

"He was also watching their webcast when we walked into his work space. At this point, it's just a data. But either way, Steve is going to watch electronic traffic in and out of Celeb-News to make sure there isn't something we're missing."

"Like what?"

Joe's eyes narrowed thoughtfully. "It's a local news company. This is the type of story that would really boost a reporter's profile, or the company's. There might be a connection there."

Tasha didn't answer, focusing instead on the road as she drove through the blistering sun towards the first house. After a few minutes of silence she cleared her throat.

"I know you're a pro and all, but I didn't bring a spare vest. I wasn't expecting to be taking doors on this trip. So I'm going to need you to hang back and when it's safe I'll call you forward."

"That won't be necessary."

"I can't put an unarmed and unarmored person in danger like that. Just hang back and you can come in when it's over."

Joe spoke slowly, choosing his words carefully. "I'm wearing my jacket, I'll be fine. If you insist, you can go first. But I must tell you, going in solo is bad tactics and violates your own rule you mentioned not ten minutes ago."

"What rule is that?"

"You won't have much of a career if you die trying to take this guy by yourself. Better to overwhelm him so there isn't much of a fight. It tends to stop the situation getting out of hand."

"I can handle myself. I've done this a few times, you know. Besides, I'm not sure how much you and your jacket are going to help," she said with a dismissive snort.

"I'm surprised you haven't noticed. My jacket is made of Brecon. It'll stop most rounds up to a .223."

"What? Nobody can afford Brecon!" She craned her neck, reaching over to feel the material and give it a tug.

"We manufacture it. In my job skill code, this is standard issue."

Tasha shook her head in disbelief. "We put in for that armor for our under-covers. Even one outfit was above our budget, and you get one as standard issue."

"The house is up ahead on the left, 300 meters," he said with a smile.

Tasha ground her teeth and sped up, turning hard into the long driveway and following it toward the back of the property. Solar panels dotted the lawn and covered the roof of a small house and the detached garage behind it. Tasha roared up to the front stoop and stopped in a cloud of dust. She climbed out of the car and walked quickly toward the porch.

"Stay put."

Joe got out of the car and leaned against it, taking in the rest of the property. Most of the trees and lawn were dead but there were multiple new wellheads scattered around the perimeter of the property. The garage was in disrepair except for a large, shiny padlock on the door. He slipped his hand casually into his pocket and waited.

Tasha hit the doorbell and peered through the windows, before rapping loudly on the door. A muffled voice inside called out and several large dogs started barking. Tasha dropped her hand down to her weapon, taking a step back from the door as it opened.

An elderly woman peered through dirty glasses at Tasha's badge, then looked over at Joe.

"Go away," she said as she jerked back into the house, trying to slam the door. Tasha reached out and stopped the door, causing the old woman to stumble awkwardly. "Go away or I'll let the dogs loose on you. I got nothing to say to you!"

"Just a couple of quick questions," Tasha said as she struggled to keep the door open without knocking the woman down. While the two of them tussled, the back door slammed open and a young Latino man took off running toward the property line.

Joe sprinted after him, overtaking him halfway across the yard. He gave the running man a shove, knocking him into a large clay pot with a single dead stalk sticking out the top.

"Going somewhere?"

The man groaned, pulling himself to a sitting position among the shards of pottery, then began to stand up to confront Joe. Looking at his size, he thought better of it and slumped back down, holding his hands up in surrender.

"What are you running from?"

The man shrugged, looking down at the dirt in silence.

"Listen, we just want to talk, and take a look in the garage," Joe said. "We can use you running as probable cause and break down the door, maybe toss the house too. Or you can just let us in. Your choice."

Tasha walked around the house, leading the old woman by the arm. Tasha walked her over to a bench and gently pushed her into a seated position. "Caught 'im, eh?"

Joe shrugged and turned away, looking at the garage. There were cameras trained on the two doors, and the dead grass shows signs of regular traffic in and out of the front door. He walked to the door and gathered himself to kick it down. The man laughed and Joe turned and stared hard at him before reaching into his pocket and clicking something.

The red lights on the cameras dimmed, the external light on the garage blinked out and the man's cell phone made several muted beeps before going silent. Joe walked slowly toward the man, never breaking eye contact.

"Perhaps you've put a trap on the door? Something else you want to mention?"

The man looked nervously around and licked his lips before replying. "You can't kick it down, its got a metal rod holding it in place."

"Show me."

The man levered himself up off the ground as the older woman rattled at him in Spanish. He lifted a sink leaning against the garage and exposed a keypad. He thumbed in a four number code and stepped back. With a loud screech, the metal rod inside retracted and the door popped open.

Joe pointed toward Tasha and stepped closer to the door, inspecting it with a small light before giving it a tentative shove. It swung open, exposing a dim room with several grow lights hanging ten feet above the ground. Joe snorted through his teeth and clicked the device in his pocket again.

The power surged back on, and the large grow lights brightened, exposing row after row of marijuana plants and a few rows of poppy plants. Joe turned away from the garage and walked back toward the car, ignoring the two residents and calling over his shoulder to Tasha.

"Wrong house, let's go."

Tasha peered into the garage and rolled her eyes before heading back to the car and climbing in. "Guess that explains all the wellheads. Don't these idiots know they can get a license?"

"What, and pay taxes? Drive."

They drove in silence as dusk settled over the valley. Joe looked through the data that Lavoy had sent him after they'd gone to the third house.

"Steve was able to take the video from our interview with Brian and extract stills from it. He's been using facial recognition software to compare the celebs on his office walls to the guest list from Helen's party."

"What video from our interview? We didn't take any video," she said, looking over at Joe in the dim light.

He tugged at the pocket of his jacket, tilting it back and forth for her to see the pinhole camera threaded through it. "Standard—"

"Standard issue, I know," Tasha interrupted with a sigh. "This is bullshit, two drug houses and a weirdo making internet videos. We've been driving all damn day."

"Could report the drug houses after this is over."

"Please, by tomorrow those sheds will be empty or burnt to the ground. I don't have jurisdiction out here in the county anyway. The sheriff could have some fun with them, though. Lean on them and get all the credit he can off them, if he even cares."

"Don't you want to know what Steve found?"

"A bunch of Hollywood hacks I'm sure."

"One in particular. Bree Sanders, a D-list celeb people pay to show up. Dabbled in a number of short-lived online shows before she got her big break on a reality called Urban Hookup. Ironically, she lost her job when they discovered she'd done numerous porn movies under a different name."

"Why do I care?" groaned Tasha. "Seriously, get to the point."

"Currently resides in the city, ex-boyfriend's residence is less than 100 meters from our fourth possible site. The gossip mags report that while she's currently dating Tuco Sanchez, she's been seen with her ex from time to time."

"You don't honestly think that moron pulled off a successful kidnapping do you?"

"Nope. But at least two of her pornos were filmed at his address, outside, in full view of the neighbor's house—which happens to be our fourth option. Carpenter had 38 different celebs on his wall, most of them matched two or three images. Bree here matched nine. Of the images on his wall, 37 were clearly taken by paparazzi or cell phones. One was taken using a telephoto lens with an expensive camera. Guess where she's standing in that photo?"

"At her ex's house?"

"Outside the house, leaning against her boyfriend's truck, talking on her phone. Do you want to know the best part?"

"There's a best part?"

"The CelebNews webcast Brian was watching when we walked in there was the after-party report from Helen Knudsen's birthday party, and the girl doing the reporting was the same girl the kidnapper emailed the ransom demand file to: Samantha West."

"How many of the photos on his wall were from stories that West was involved in?"

"All of them. Also, her previous job was as a reporter for a small anti-corporate outfit in San Francisco. She wasn't there long, but she did interview numerous startup employees in the area, focusing on the poor work–life balance, low pay and frequent outsourcing of their jobs once the company has started. One of her last stories involved employees of *Zoom! Personal Valet Service*, with the lead references being Mina Kyper and Brian Carpenter."

"Our suspect knows a reporter who was at Helen's party?" Tasha subconsciously reached for her phone before remembering it wasn't there.

"She was the one who gave Helen the cab vouchers, and she's the one Brian's been sending information to."

"Did Steve figure out who owns the house next door? Tell me it's not West or somebody she knows."

"Jacob Kyper, age 54, and his daughter Mina Kyper, age 26. Mina was something of a local prodigy, graduating from college Magna Cum Laude with degrees in programming and math, and a number of peer reviewed papers on optimized routes to her credit. Guess what her first job at *Zoom!* was."

Tasha gradually accelerated the car, her lips pressed in a narrow line. "Tell me."

"She was one of the original architects of the program. She developed the autonomous routing algorithm. Seven months ago she tendered her resignation via email, stating she felt like she'd missed out on being young and needed a break from all the pressure, so she was going on a cutting the cord trip, no technology. Since then she's had zero social media presence. There have been occasional purchases on her credit cards, the last one in Kenya. Having spent some time in Kenya in the last seven months, I can say without any reasonable doubt that nobody looking to relax would head there."

"And Jacob, what about him?" Tasha said.

"House bills are still auto-debited from his accounts. No

social media profile, but phone and internet activity to the house continue. Nothing of else note."

Tasha swore under her breath, gripping the wheel tightly. Her breathing slowed and she squinted ahead as darkness fell.

"How far to the house?"

"Three miles or so, and then it's about a quarter mile back from the road."

She immediately pulled the car over on the side of the road carefully, turning the lights off and putting the car in park. She flipped the map book open and held a small light over it, and Joe held up the satellite imagery of the house.

"The property has a house and detached pole barn, plus that shed off in the back corner. That looks new."

"Well the image of the house was from several months ago, so it was new then."

"Right, whatever. We're going to pull into this field a half mile past the house and approach from the rear. I'll head to the house, you check out the barn. Do you think you can use one of your fancy toys to gain access without tripping any alarms?"

"Depends on the alarm."

"For all your talk, that's the best you can do?" she snorted at him.

"There are no certainties in life."

She sketched rapidly on her notepad.

"So you approach from the south, scale this shitty fence and check out the barn. I'll come in from the west and check out the house. If you do trip an alarm, at least it will draw him to you and that should give me the element of surprise."

"Assuming he's not in the barn, yes."

She drew another line from the barn to the house.

"There were some hedges through here. If the barn is a dud, you can use them as cover to meet me at the house and we'll decide what to do next. We need to get going or else the moon will be up and we'll be exposed."

Joe grunted his agreement and went back to studying the satellite image. Tasha put the car in gear and veered down the road toward the house, heart pounding with anticipation.

CHAPTER EIGHT

Tasha crept softly through the field, dry grass and weeds crunching beneath her feet. The moon was just starting to show overhead, illuminating the fence surrounding the yard.

She paused, searching to the south for any sign of Joe. A shadow that might be a man or might be a tree, an owl swooping across the field, and the stark shadows of dead plants were all she could see. She shook her head—he'd left her at the car without a word. No last-minute condescending advice, even. One moment he was there, bag over his shoulder, and the next moment he was gone.

"Spooky," she muttered, reaching for the fence post and carefully sliding a leg over the fence in the sparse cover of a dead bush. She'd almost made it over the wire when the top strand grazed her inner thigh, sending a powerful jolt of electricity into her body. Her muscles seized and she dropped heavily to the ground, clutching her leg in agony. She lay still for several minutes, fighting back tears as the pain gradually subsided.

She studied the fence from her spot on the ground, noting that a third wire had been threaded through the barbed wire, and that the wire insulators at the post had been painted matte black. She groaned, rolled onto her belly and pulled her weapon.

"No way that fence is legal voltage," she said into the dirt. Grunting, she scrambled to her feet and did an awkward crouch-run across the barren yard to the side of the house, pausing when she reached the shadows to stuff her hand down her pants and feel around gingerly. She winced in pain when her fingers found the blister forming where the wire had touched her.

She pulled her hand free and looked toward the barn, scanning for any sign of Joe. Through the wall, she heard the music playing and a heavy rhythmic thumping. She leaned her head against the wall and listened hard.

The repetitive thumping came in rapid bursts with an occasional louder, deeper sound. In the background, she thought she could make out a female voice, somewhat distressed.

Jerking away from the wall, Tasha stole another look around the corner at the barn—still no sign of Joe.

She inched her way down the length of the house, toward the front door, looking in the windows as she went. She couldn't make out any signs of disturbance. The living room was dark, but everything seemed in place—family pictures lining the walls, dinner table set for two, and some flowers, past their prime, in a vase on the counter.

Satisfied there was nobody near the front of the house, Tasha worked her way back toward the barn, peering through windows again as she went. Through the bathroom window she could see female makeup neatly arranged on the sink, bright pink towels hanging from the racks. Several faded toy unicorns rested on the inside windowsill. The noise inside grew louder. The girl's voice was intermittent now, and softer.

Tasha approached another window, licking her lips and

trying to calm her pounding heart. The shades were drawn, but she could see inside through the gaps between the blinds. Light from the hallway shone through the open doorway, illuminating a neat bedroom, unremarkable except for a dark shape on the wall opposite the bed. Tasha crept past the window and looked in at a different angle, struggling to make out what it was. She cautiously shone the narrow beam of her flashlight into the room for an instant and gasped as the realization hit her. Near the edge of the bed stood a tripod, illuminated in the light and casting the shadow on the wall; the camera on the tripod was pointed toward an open closet.

The light from the hallway dimmed momentarily as someone walked down the hall, and Tasha ducked away from the window, clutching her handgun. Beads of sweat formed on her brow as she listened intently for footsteps or voices.

After a few minutes of silence, she peered into the room again. Seeing nothing, she moved back toward the barn, poking her head around the corner of the house. The barn was still, no sign of Joe or any other activity. She leaned back around the corner, gathering herself before creeping toward the French doors that led into the living room from the side of the house. She inched up to the doorjamb, scanning the room for any signs of life.

The room was still empty. She took a small metal shim out of her pocket and slipped it between the door and the locking mechanism, feeling around for the latch and then quietly forcing it upward.

The lock disengaged with a sound loud enough to wake the dead, and she jerked away from the door, doing her best to blend in with the shadows. She held her breath, but all she could hear was the steady thumping noise. There was nothing from the girl now.

She eased the door open and waited again, watching the

hallway for any signs of movement. The sounds continued from the rear of the house, culminating in a loud shriek.

Lifting her weapon, Tasha started into the house. The thumping noise now replaced by electronic music and an indistinct bass voice. She was at the threshold to the kitchen when a rapidly approaching shadow caused her to freeze in her tracks.

Brian came stomping down the hallway, tossing an empty energy drink can in the trash before yanking the fridge door open and grabbing another one.

"So much bullshit, no way that bastard got me…" he muttered. He popped the lid and shuffled back toward the hallway. His steps faltered as he caught sight of Tasha in the shadows. For a split second they stared at each other, an arm's length apart.

"Police. You are under arrest," Tasha said loudly.

Brian dodged to her right and sprayed the energy drink in her eyes. Momentarily blinded, she didn't see him bull rush her until he'd knocked her gun hand into the cabinet and driven his shoulder into her vest.

The gun discharged into the wall, and was knocked out of her hand as he rammed her backwards into the dining room table, snatching the vase off the counter and smashing it against her head. She raised her arms over her face as he leaned in, pinning her to the table and pummeling her arms and shoulders with wild punches.

She blocked most of his blows, but occasionally he snuck one through, hitting her head and forcing it down against the wood of the table. With a fearsome jerk, she managed to unpin her leg and used it to lever him away. He crashed into the wall, knocking down several pictures. Reaching back over her head, she grabbed one of the place settings and hurled it at him. The heavy plate bounced off his head and shattered on the floor as he charged back in.

Tasha kicked out viciously with her boot, catching him high in the left shoulder before he could set his feet, and he tumbled backward again. Regaining his balance, he lobbed a stained glass lamp at her head, forcing her to block the shot and shatter it with her forearm.

She cried out, clutching her arm and kicking one of the chairs into his path as he lunged for the hallway. He tumbled to the ground, crushing a yellow tin trashcan and rolling into the kitchen. Stumbling to his feet, Brian cursed and began throwing kitchen knives. The first stuck in her vest before falling heavily, gashing her thigh. She stumbled into the counter, the next knife narrowly missing her, driving instead into the stereo in the living room.

Desperate, Tasha snatched a toaster off the counter and hurled it at him. He picked up a third knife and Tasha knocked it out of his hand. Brian grabbed the toaster's cord, swung it over his head, and it grazed the ceiling fan before hitting her in the shoulder. She closed the distance, punching him repeatedly in the face, then lifting her boot and stomping the heel on his bare foot. He screamed, grabbing at her hair as he fell and pulling her with him into a tangle on the floor.

He punched at her chest and stomach, hitting her vest while she tried to use her good forearm to put him in a chokehold. Grabbing a shard of the broken plate, he began stabbing her thigh and calf, slamming his head back into her face until he connected and she heard a sickening crunch on the bridge of her nose.

She sprawled away from him onto her side and he sprang to his feet, aiming a wicked kick at her head. She took the brunt of the kick with her mangled forearm. A piece of glass still stuck in her arm opened a cut on the bottom his foot. He howled in pain, instinctively lifting his knee to grab his foot.

Seizing her chance, Tasha grabbed the edge of the cabinets

and used them as leverage to spin her body on the bloody tiles, sweeping out his standing leg with a boot to the side of his knee. He dropped to the floor, splintering a cabinet door with his head on the way down.

He lay there, dazed, spitting blood and trying to slide away from her, convulsing. Tasha wrested herself up on her good arm, coughing up blood and tucking the pieces of skin hanging off her arm back into her shirt. She heard the crunch of a boot on glass and looked up apprehensively.

Standing above her was a man dressed in dark clothes, a mask and thermal goggles over his eyes, holding her weapon. Without a word he lifted the gun and fired twice, sending bullets into Brian's gut. Casually, he forced the gun to stovepipe a round and tossed it back into the living room, then pulled his own gun before walking down the hallway.

"Joe! I had him, Joe. What the hell are you doing?"

Joe didn't answer. He walked down the hall, skirting around the knife she had knocked from Brian's hand and pausing at the bullet hole left by her first shot. He reached a gloved hand over and opened the door, shining a bright strobe light inside. He stood there, silently assessing the room as it was intermittently lit by the light. Then he turned and walked further up the hallway.

Tasha crawled into the living room and looked around for her gun. When she found it, she saw the round jammed in the chamber and tried to clear it. As she pulled on the slide with her injured arm, the exertion caused her muscles and tendons to grate on the shards of glass and she let out a shriek of pain. She flipped over on her back, breathing heavily. She braced the gun's slide against it her boot, racking it hard and ejecting the jammed round. She used the broken dining chair nearby to pull herself up and stumbled through the living room to the kitchen, looking down at Brian as she passed.

He sat wedged in the corner of the kitchen, blood pumping out of his abdomen. His eyes slowly tracked up toward Tasha, and their stares locked. His lips curled into a sneer.

"What if I had been innocent? Then what?"

"But you aren't," she slurred.

"You have no idea," he said, breaking into a coughing laugh that sprayed blood on the fridge and peppered the walls. "Even from prison, I will haunt you."

He continued to laugh as she walked down the hallway leaving a trail of blood in her wake, the sound echoing loudly and sending chills down her spine. She reached the door Joe had paused at, braced herself on the doorframe and fumbled around inside for the light switch. A flood of light filled the room, and her breath caught in her throat at the site.

There was no furniture, only a single blanket on the floor. A large aerial photo of the Knudsen estate, probably taken by a small drone, covered most of one wall. The image showed the surrounding neighborhoods, gradually moving from lush greens and robust trees to drought stricken brown patches. Surrounding the image were hundreds of photographs of impoverished people from many countries, their flat eyes staring over at the image of the estate.

The image bored into Tasha's mind as she worked up the courage to look down at the blanket. Huddled beneath it was the shape of a woman, her bare feet zip-tied together and protruding from the hem.

In the center of the blanket, there was a small hole, a red stain spreading around it. Tasha fell to her knees, gasping in pain, eyes fixed on the single bullet hole in the wall. She winced and rolled the girl over.

She stared into the lifeless blue eyes of Helen Knudsen. The girl's mascara had run down her cheeks, her lipstick was smeared down one side of her face, the slightest hint of blood on her lips.

Tasha sat back, pushing away from Helen and leaning against the wall, a ragged breath escaping her mouth as tears began to stream down her face. She sat, unable to move, until she was stirred by a girl's voice in the back of the house—the same panicked cries she'd heard earlier.

She struggled to her feet, gripping the doorjamb and launching herself into the hallway. She staggered down the hall, still trailing blood, until she found the source of the noise. The door was open and she pushed inside, waving her gun into each corner as she struggled to stay upright.

A console game cut screen played across the TV in the corner, displaying a gruesomely mangled body on an urban street. The screen showed blood and shell casings scattered everywhere. In one corner of the image, a woman sat tied up in a chair waiting to be rescued. Every few minutes she would beg for somebody to help her, pleading with the dead player's character to save her. At the end of each stream of dialogue, she screamed in horror.

Joe sat at a desk in the opposite corner, typing on a keyboard, several portable disk drives hooked into an array of servers in front of him. Empty pizza boxes and snack food were stacked neatly behind the couch, the only wall decoration a massive poster of Che Guevara.

"Joe, what... what are you doing?"

"Cleaning up this mess. He has a lot of data on Knudsen, surveillance data, bank data, it seems like he's been watching him for a while."

"What?"

"I'm stripping his servers and then we're going to sanitize this place before the sheriff gets here. Before we call him, I have somebody else coming to help us."

"Helen's dead," Tasha said quietly.

"Yes, by your hand it would appear. Then again, the only person who can say you shot her should be about dead by now," Joe said, checking his watch.

"What?"

"Brian, the instigator of this drama, should have bled out by now, unless his liver is located somewhere else. That means the only person who can contradict your story that he took your gun and fired it into the wall to kill Helen as you were fighting—should be about dead."

Tasha leaned against the wall, staring dully at Joe's back. For a brief moment she considered pointing her gun at him, but she lacked the strength.

"Except you. You could still tell the truth."

"Detective, I was never here."

"You said it yourself. Nobody would believe me if I said I investigated out in the county alone."

A crunch of glass from the other room startled Tasha, and she stumbled away from the doorway, dropping her gun. Joe continued typing, apparently unfazed. Moments later a man walked in, very similar in appearance and stature to Joe, wearing clothes almost identical to those that Joe had been dressed in earlier that night.

"Damn man, you really tore that guy up," the man said while he took in the room, casually toeing Tasha's gun away from her outstretched hand.

"That's her handiwork." Joe replied, nodding his head in Tasha's direction but otherwise remaining fixed on the computer screen.

"Who's this guy?" Tasha asked quietly, her lips trembling with uncertainty.

"This is your new partner. He is a private investigator, goes by the name of Joe. He works for a small firm that Helen's father hired. He will be your witness to tonight's mess, your alibi, and most importantly, he will replace me."

"Let me guess, because you were never here?"

"I'm too busy to be tied up in a court case. So our friend here will do all the paperwork. He's what you might call a professional witness, and since you made a bit of a hash of apprehending our suspect, there is undoubtedly going to be a court case. Or at the very least a lot of tedious media interviews."

"This is such bullshit."

"This is the reality of your situation. If you fight it, the truth comes out, and you'll be publically ousted as the person who carelessly shot Helen Knudsen and then executed Brian to cover it up. You'll recall I tried to help, but you sent me on a wild goose chase so you could enter the house alone in the hope of saving all the glory for yourself."

Joe turned around and tapped the part of his jacket where he'd shown her the camera earlier.

"Standard issue, remember? I caught your rant in the car on film before we hit that first house, making sure I knew to stay out of your way and that you would handle it without me. Careless words, Ms. Strauss."

Tasha spat a mess of blood on the floor. "Where the hell did you go? You left me outside the house alone, never made an effort to get to the house until I was already inside, beat half to death. It can't have taken you that long to scope the barn. I've seen the crap in your bag, that should have been a cakewalk."

"I came after you started shooting the place up. Before that I was searching the barn, as we agreed."

"And how did you get here so fast?" She swiveled to look at the new Joe.

"I've been following your progress for two days. Preparation in case it went bad. Our employer believes in contingency planning."

"Well maybe if you'd helped it wouldn't have gone bad in the first place."

Joe typed a few final keystrokes and the screens blinked, powering down. He stood up and packed the hard drives into his bag. He walked down the hall and out of the house without a word.

The new Joe extended a hand down to her. "Come on, let's get you somewhere you can sit down comfortably and make sure we have our story down before the sheriff gets here."

Grudgingly she took his hand and dragged herself upright, looking once more at the TV as it flashed a message signifying the end of the game.

Mission Failed: Objectives Not Met

Tasha leaned back on the gurney and let the nurse do her work. Blood loss was rapidly sapping her strength and she felt dazed. She watched through eyes nearly swollen shut as the sheriff's tactical team and crime scene investigators swarmed the house and surrounding area, searching for any more perpetrators.

A strong hand grabbed her wrist and held her still, and she felt an IV needle prick her arm. She mumbled a weak protest, turning her head to look at the nurse, her eyes widening as she realized it was the same nurse she'd seen in Knudsen's office during their initial meeting. She started to sit up, but the woman firmly pressed her back into the gurney, pulling a strap across her chest and working to clean her arm.

"Relax. Just an IV with some medication and fluids. You need it. You practically painted that house with blood."

"I know who you are," she croaked, straining slightly against the restraints.

"Good, then you know you're getting top quality care, now shut up and relax. I didn't get dragged way out in the sticks to have you spraying me with blood because you can't appreciate a stroke of good fortune when it hits you."

Tasha groaned as the woman gingerly extracted a long sliver of glass and put it in an evidence bag. Two men approached from the edge of Tasha's vision, the sheriff and another man. As they stepped into the light she let out another groan, this time of resignation as she realized the second man was Steve Lavoy, the corporate fixer.

"Will she be okay?" the sheriff asked softly.

"Yes, barring some bad luck with an antibiotic resistant bug or something like that. Most of the damage is superficial. Just the same, she should be held at the hospital for a few days, and they'll need to scan for internal damage. But so far, it's just a broken nose, possibly some fractured ribs, about a hundred stitches and counting. I've got some clotting agent on the stab wounds and gash in her leg and I'm working on her arms now. Be another forty minutes, or we can stabilize her and get her to a hospital now," the nurse said, as she focused on pulling the glass from Tasha's arm.

"She'll get better care from her," Lavoy said with a nod toward the nurse.

The sheriff nodded. "Up to you, Detective. I'd let her take care of you for the externals and then head to the hospital for the rest. But it's your call." He turned his head toward Lavoy and put a hand on his shoulder. "I want you to know the sheriff's office appreciates your support and assistance in this matter. Your company has always been helpful in situations like this."

"I know how the budget cuts of the last few years have taken their toll. Our company stands ready to support law enforcement. Whenever you need help, feel free to call. We consider it a civic duty above all else. Tonight we got lucky—our aid may have prevented her having to endure a long and painful recovery, maybe even saved her life."

The sheriff gave Tasha's shin a sympathetic squeeze and walked away with Lavoy, intermittent fragments of their conversation about a diminishing tax base and drought-stricken economy drifting back to her on the wind. She gave a resigned sigh and looked around.

The new Joe was giving a detailed report, taking the sheriff's deputies around the lot and pointing out the timeline. She noticed he had her actual movements down precisely, indicating where she encountered the electric fence and how she moved up and down the siding of the house. The deputies dutifully followed along, taping off sections of the property and bringing in lights to illuminate specific areas. They were paying particular attention to the trampled brown grass along the house and the impact point where she fell crossing the fence line.

A tactical team breached the door to the barn and entered. After several minutes they reemerged and declared the building secure. Tasha's vision went hazy as the painkillers kicked in and she turned her head toward the nurse.

"You drugged me," she slurred at her.

"Yep, officially nothing you say tonight will matter. Between your injuries and the medication, any errors in your story will be overlooked."

"No decency..."

The nurse looked up from Tasha's arm, peering through her safety glasses. Her breath crystalized in the cold night air. For a long moment she stared at Tasha as though trying to discern something from her face. Tasha saw her reflection in the safety glasses—cuts all over her face, eyes swelling shut and blood in her hair. Tears welled painfully in her eyes, mixing with caked blood and dripping slowly down her face.

"Rarely does decency appear in our lines of work," the nurse said kindly, reaching a gloved hand up to wipe a tear away.

The forensics team began pushing carts of equipment into the barn as the last of the tactical team cleared out. The first cart cleared the threshold of the doorway, settling heavily onto the floor. The tech gave it a shove, stepping into the building after it. Suddenly, a brilliant flash lit up the night sky and the ground heaved sharply as the entry to the barn exploded.

The tech and two of the tactical team were thrown clear of the door, landing in a jumbled pile in the dust beyond, limbs fractured and twisted out of place. Police across the crime scene dropped what they were doing and raced to the barn, calling for medics. They surrounded the downed men in a tight cluster, working frantically to try to stop the bleeding.

"Go help them. Please." Tasha murmured.

The nurse stood stock still, watching the scene at the other end of the property, a grim look in her eyes.

"I'm going to move you back. In my experience, there's always a second bomb."

She kicked the brakes on the gurney and gave it a heave, pushing it behind a parked SUV before returning to retrieve her folding table and equipment. She ripped her gloves off and put on a head lamp, before getting new gloves and calmly resuming work on Tasha.

"Help them, you have to help them, I'm fine here. But—"

"Lie still," she said firmly, planting a hand on Tasha's chest and forcing her down while tightening the restraint. "I was brought here to care for you, not them. I do what I'm told and I haven't been told to get involved in a bombing. Now—"

A second explosion lit the sky, this one larger, and a fireball rose high above the buildings. The nurse leaped forward, shielding Tasha's open wounds with her body as a wave of dust and debris washed over the area, breaking the rear window of the SUV and peppering the ground with impacts. The nurse held her position until the dust began to settle, then stood back upright and carefully wiped the debris off Tasha's face.

As the cries of the wounded reached their ears, she looked up and said sadly, "Like I said, always two bombs."

Sirens wailed, bringing additional medics to the scene. Tasha drifted out of consciousness.

CHAPTER NINE

The soft beep of the monitor stirred Tasha awake. She was in a single occupancy hospital room. The TV, still on since before she'd passed out, was airing news coverage of the Helen Knudsen tragedy. The station had a panel of experts discussing the nature of kidnappers, with footage of the media scrum outside the Knudsen mansion playing in the background.

She shifted her weight awkwardly, and a dull ache pulsed through her body to her puffy face. A thin dribble of fluid leaked out of her stitches and down her cheek. Her movement drew the attention of the desk nurse, who picked up a phone and called for another nurse to come and attend to her.

"How are we feeling today Ms. Strauss?" the nurse asked cheerfully.

Tasha nodded her head, wincing as the motion caused pain to rush into her brain.

"I feel terrible," she finally managed. "But I could stand to eat."

"Of course. We'll have some food brought in right away.

The nurse smiled and walked out of the room. Tasha turned the sound up on the TV so she could hear the panel. A social media tracking banner scrolled across the bottom of the screen, viewer feedback indicating that people felt the police had failed Helen Knudsen. The panel shifted gears and started discussing the shootout and bombing at the ranch.

She tilted her bed forward and turned the volume up in interest. The lead reporter was questioning a former FBI agent.

"So the sheriff indicated in a press conference two days ago that the police department had requested the ATF and FBI to assist the State CID in handling the scene. What new dimension does this add to the investigation?"

"Well, obviously bringing in federal resources on a case like this is a good thing. These outlying counties have been hit hard by years of budget pressure, and dealing with a crime scene of this magnitude is going to be difficult. By all accounts the person responsible for Helen Knudsen's death was killed during the confrontation, so the possibility that they'll find new evidence that leads to a third party is unlikely."

A former state prosecutor chimed in. *"I disagree. I think that the inclusion of the Feds in this case will help determine the extent of the perpetrator's criminal activity. It seems unlikely that this is the suspect's first serious offense.. The fact that six members of the sheriff's department died in the bombing, after the suspect was neutralized, will only add urgency to the investigation."*

"Six dead," Tasha murmured.

"While I agree the casualties will bring a great deal of scrutiny onto this incident, we've not seen evidence to suggest..."

"Hold on. Sorry to interrupt, gentlemen, but I believe we have some breaking news." The reporter interrupted. They all turned to the screens behind the dais. *"Yes, we have some live video being broadcast right now. We're going to put it up on the screens. Let's watch."*

The screen lit up, footage showing police standing around

the *Zoom!* maintenance depot questioning the workers and poking around the vehicle bays, before cutting to a new scene—the police chasing the autonomous cab through heavily crowded streets, bumping civilian cars out of the way and causing numerous crashes. Finally, there was an edited scene that appeared to show police cars crashing through the park, hitting pedestrians. The video slowed down and looped through that final scene multiple times.

"That's not how it happened," Tasha said weakly. Her monitor began beeping faster.

The video ended with the cops standing around the cab as it was pulled out of the duck pond, Captain Jackson and the two lead detectives talking calmly as though nothing had happened. The time stamps on the footage had been altered to make it seem as though they had only been there for minutes rather than showing up an hour later, when the injured had been cared for and the scene secured. Of her efforts to break the window on the cab there was nothing, nor was there anything showing Joe's presence.

Text began to scroll slowly across the screen in a cheerful font.

The police cannot protect you—this is the best they had to offer. A police captain known to be politically connected, a lead detective who failed to pass the detective's exam three times, and as backup, a man with two excessive violence complaints against him, including one for punching a teenager that mouthed off at him. They won't ever find me.

The video ended with a still frame of Helen Knudsen sitting on a blanket in her underwear, blindfolded and bound. The image faded slowly to black.

"I suppose it's little solace to know that these videos were planted on the net to release automatically at prescheduled intervals. There's no accomplice," Captain Jackson said as he walked in and closed the door.

Tasha turned her head slowly toward him, rage in her eyes. "How can you be sure? Toward the end of our investigation there was strong evidence linking Brian Carpenter to Samantha West, a CelebNews reporter."

"He had the ranch rigged up with surveillance cameras, some inside, most of them outside. We've got video of him for weeks before the kidnapping up through the explosion at the barn. She never shows up on any of it."

Tasha's stomach tightened when she realized the entire episode at the ranch had been caught on film. Jackson was watching the TV and didn't notice her agitation, so she regained her composure before speaking again.

"So that means you have video of what happened the night we confronted him."

"For the most part. Some of the cameras seemed to have suffered intermittent power failures during the night. The house was heavily damaged by the explosion, but even before that, the FBI suspects all the fighting you guys did in the kitchen and living room may have jarred a few wires loose. Having said that, most of the fight in the kitchen was caught. Right up until he started throwing knives at you. That was a hell of a fight. There's a debate going as to whether we should release that footage as part of damage control for the pain the media is putting us through," Jackson said, jerking his head at the TV.

"I'd rather you didn't."

"My feelings as well. Not just for you, but showing you confronting him alone won't do us any favors. The media is pounding us for not getting enough bodies on the problem as it is."

"And Joe, what about him? Does he get a pass on all of this?"

Jackson paused, looking down at her bandaged legs. "I believe the situation with Joe will be taken care of. I trust you are sensitive to how that needs to be handled."

"That depends."

"On what?"

"Whose bomb that was."

"Well that you can rest easy on. Preliminary results from the FBI lab came back with trace evidence indicating our suspect built the first bomb. He had it rigged to a pressure plate in the door threshold that activated if you didn't put the right code in the keypad. He might be a brilliant coder, but he wasn't terribly proficient at bomb making. They think he rigged the plate wrong and it didn't recognize that somebody was standing on it until they put that big dolly full of gear on it."

"He killed six people with that bomb, I'd call that proficient."

"Most of them died in the secondary blast. The first blast killed the tech and mangled the two entry men, but didn't do much beyond that. Pretty simple device, pressure cooker packed with nails; the officers were protected by their armor for the most part. The tech wasn't so lucky. The second blast doesn't appear to have been planned. He had a large stash of flammable materials and battery units for the cars stored in the barn. When the first bomb went off, the back blast tore into some of the containers. It didn't take a very big spark to blow it. Did a number on the southwest part of the barn and shredded the back of the house."

"What about his computers? All the data..."

"FBI is trying to sift through it. A number of large metal pieces flew right through the room, taking out much of his setup. The room we found Helen in was pretty much the only room in the house that didn't end up trashed from either the explosions or you punching your way through every decoration in the place."

"Son of a bitch."

"Easy. Right now, Knudsen's friends at the KSI are backing up your story to the hilt. They produced a bunch of profiling evidence of the suspect and gave it to the FBI, and the walk-through Joe gave the detectives is spot on with the surveillance footage. Everything tracks to the story. Let's not muddy the waters because you're mad at him."

"He was out of my sight around the barn for a long time, he could have rigged any number of—"

"Enough," Jackson said kindly. "The crime lab puts hair, prints and even a small amount of blood from the suspect on the bomb device in the doorway. It's enough for them. Be smart and don't stir the pot. This is on the edge of going bad for the department as it is."

A knock at the door interrupted them before Tasha could respond, and in walked Steve Lavoy with a basket of flowers.

"Glad to see you're feeling better, Detective," he said.

"Thanks." Her eyes narrowed as she studied him closely. "Nice jacket. Standard issue, I assume?"

"Of course. Perfect for any unexpected surprises," Lavoy responded dryly.

Jackson looked at the two of them quizzically, but stayed silent.

"Six dead at the ranch, but you look like you escaped without a scratch," Tasha said.

"Yes, although it's eight dead at the ranch if you count the victim and the suspect. Fortunately, we were sheltered by the shed in the back when the explosion hit."

"Convenient."

Lavoy arched an eyebrow at her and shot a sideways glance at Jackson. "Lucky, that's all."

"And the sheriff?" Tasha prodded.

"Shaken up. He caught a bit of shrapnel during the second explosion, but it didn't hit him anywhere vital. He was fit enough for the press conference the next morning, even had a fresh uniform on."

"What can we help you with, Mr. Lavoy?" Jackson asked patiently.

"Just stopping by to see how Ms. Strauss is doing, Captain. With gratitude, and in honor of your sacrifice, we're covering your medical expenses during your stay in the hospital, and any physical therapy afterward."

"Thanks," Tasha said without enthusiasm.

"We have also upgraded your food coverage, which should be arriving shortly. I wish you a speedy recovery, Detective. I hope our next meeting is under better circumstances."

Lavoy walked out the door, holding it open as an orderly brought in a cart carrying something that smelled delicious.

"Good afternoon, Detective. My name is Julio. I'll be arranging your food for you during your hospital stay. We have arranged for you to have a few of your personal favorites available."

"And how do you know my personal favorites?"

"Steadfast investigative work, Detective. Have a good day!" Lavoy called from the doorway, before he walked swiftly down the hall to the elevator.

"Ms. Strauss." Julio uncovered the first dish. "We have two soups—a clam chowder and a chicken noodle soup. Here, we have lobster ravioli with a light red sauce, a salad and fruit cocktail. On this plate, three mahi tacos with cheese, no onions. And for dessert, there are freshly baked peanut butter cookies. What would you like to start with?"

Tasha took in the tantalizing smells through her mangled

nose and broke into a smile. "Care to join me Captain? Not sure I can eat all of this."

Jackson hesitated, looking back at the TV screen as the panel discussed his future after such a colossal failure. Eventually the delicious aroma got to him.

"Sure, Tasha. I'd like nothing better."

A brush of air past her face and the click of a lock being thrown pulled Tasha from her nightmare. She lay in the dark, eyes cracked, scanning the room in alarm as her hand inched toward the call button.

A shadow detached itself from the far wall and moved swiftly to her side, snatching the alarm out of her grasp and placing a hand gently over her mouth. Another shadow bracketed her on the other side of the bed and leaned in, his breath coming in shallow rasps. The first man leaned forward into the dim light and put a finger to his lips, holding out a badge for her to inspect.

She could make out the bold letters of an FBI badge, and moved her head silently in understanding. The man holding her mouth relaxed and motioned to his partner, who began scanning the room with a small device.

The first agent carefully pulled a chair to the bed and leaned in, his slate gray eyes peering out from thin wire-framed glasses. He whispered, almost inaudibly, "Give us just a second to check for anything out of the ordinary."

Tasha lay as still as possible while the other agent, a short man with a thick mustache scanned the room meticulously. As he neared the window his device lit up, and after several passes over the area he found the bug. He took another small instrument out of his pocket, suction-cupped it to the glass near the bug and turned it on. He finished his sweep before giving a satisfied nod to gray-eyes.

"As long as we talk softly, we should be fine. It seems somebody has an interest in what you have to say these days. That makes us curious. We have some questions about recent events, questions best asked in the early morning hours. Do you understand?"

"Yes."

"I'm Agent Casey Hopper. That's Agent Mike Sullivan."

"First off, a few questions. The man who briefed the sheriff and his people is not the same man you were working with. I'm not interested in the person who talked to the sheriff, but the other person. What name did he give?"

Tasha started, her eyes widening ever so slightly. Hopper smirked.

"Joe. He said his name was Joe."

Hopper exchanged a knowing glance with Sullivan.

"Did he mention anything about Africa, perhaps Kenya specifically?"

"No. Oh wait, yes he did. He said he'd been to Kenya recently or something like that. I don't remember the context exactly, it was an offhand remark."

"That's our boy," Sullivan said in satisfaction.

"Maybe. Hard to say for sure yet." Hopper turned back to Tasha. "Would you say he acted like a typical private investigator? Or did he seem... exceptional in any way?"

"There was nothing normal about him. Do you know the difference between a dog and a wolf? A wolf stalks and hunts with intensity; a dog does its job. It's hard to explain—almost a predatory feel. His gear, his methods and his thinking are focused on... I don't know. Big game. At first I underestimated him, I didn't think I needed him. Near the end..." Her eyes glazed over as she thought about that final encounter at the house. She shook her head and looked at Hopper. "At no point did he need me for anything other than the official face of the investigation, I know that now."

Hopper took a moment to digest her statement, looking at Sullivan who was furiously scribbling notes. He rubbed his hand thoughtfully across his chin, the light stubble rasping in the silence.

"I'm going to show you some pictures, I want you to tell me if you recognize anyone."

He pulled a small electronic display out of his pocket and slowly flipped through photos. Finally, after a half dozen went past, she pointed at the screen.

"That's Joe. That's who was with me at the ranch."

Hopper didn't respond immediately, staring at the screen with her a moment longer before he sent the image to Sullivan's device. Several more images went past before she indicated another person.

"I know him—Steve Lavoy. He was the person who first met us at Knudsen's house, and he showed up at the ranch. He also brought me those flowers."

"Yes, we know him. Slippery operator, as near as we can tell, he's—" Hopper's glare caused Sullivan's voice to trail off. He continued to flip through pictures before she stopped him again.

"I saw this man also."

Hopper started. He looked between Tasha and the picture, his eyes hardening. "You are positive you've seen this man?"

She hesitated briefly before nodding her head with conviction. "Yes, I saw him at the park after the car chase."

Hopper and Sullivan were visibly disturbed. They stared at each other in silence as if debating what to do. She reached over and tugged on Hopper's arm.

"What? What's the matter?"

"Nothing to be concerned about."

"Bullshit, I'm not stupid. I need to know why you look scared."

"I'm not scared," Hopper spat out defensively.

"I need to know. I need to know my life isn't in danger because I talked to you," Tasha pleaded.

After a long pause Hopper relented. "That's a ghost. I filled the photo array with people we've seen and people who have been out of action a long time, to discern what you could remember accurately. The person you identified is a mystery. About the time we became interested in Joe, their paths intersected. Reports are that he died in Africa, when Joe was there. I only added him because he was known to have dealt with Joe. What context did you see him in? Was he helping Joe? Was he observing?"

"I just saw him for a second. He had a small dog on a leash, near the dog park where the cab crashed."

"Did he and Joe see each other?"

"I was a little busy," Tasha said dryly. "I noticed him staring at Joe like he wanted to talk to him as I was wading out of the water, after we discovered Helen wasn't in the cab."

Hopper looked up at Sullivan. "Coincidence?"

"What are the odds? I mean seriously. What are the odds that a random stranger crashes the cab into the pond right next to that guy?"

"Who is he?"

Hopper ignored her. "You don't think the suspect tried to kill him with the cab do you? How would he even know where to find him? Why would he care?"

"Maybe Carpenter is not so random after all?"

"Who is this guy?" Tasha said, alarm creeping into her voice.

"He goes off grid for over a year and suddenly pops up walking a dog next to a car accident caused by an unrelated kidnapping?" Hopper said to Mike. "We need surveillance for everything around that park. We need to be certain before we raise any hell."

Tasha reached up and grabbed Hopper's shoulder, pulling him close and whispering urgently in his face. "Who. Is. He?"

Hopper pulled away irritably. He looked over at Sullivan and got a shrug in response. "His name is John Hatfield. He used to be a spook."

"And then?"

"He died. They sent reports back he was killed in Africa. His family held a funeral; he got a star on the wall at Langley. He's ancient history."

"Clearly not," Tasha said with some amusement.

Hopper leaned in close, clenching her bicep in his grip. "For your safety, I wouldn't repeat any of this to anyone. If Hatfield's alive, this could put a whole new spin on why this kidnapping happened in the first place. Maybe Knudsen wasn't the target. If he wasn't the target and Hatfield was... I'm not sure what that means."

"It seems unlikely. I don't buy this guy went after Knudsen to get to Hatfield. Hell, I don't buy he was in a park with some glorified lapdog, even. But it does explain why the company would lift its finger to help Knudsen."

"What do you mean?" Hopper asked.

Sullivan glanced at Tasha then continued. "Let's play the 'what if?' game. We know what supposedly happened to Hatfield. Captured by Islamic militants, tortured and murdered. We know Joe went to Africa for some reason or other. If he went there and rescued Hatfield, or bought him back or whatever, Hatfield might work for them now. If that's the case, it makes sense. I mean, they have a big facility in town and a bunch of smaller ones scattered through the countryside. Maybe he works at one of them."

"How does that explain him being at the accident scene?"

"That park is less than a mile from their veteran's assistance center. Maybe he's been recovering there and walked over for some peace and quiet. Who knows?"

Hopper swore under his breath and put his display away. "You know if that's Hatfield..."

"If that's Hatfield, we're swimming in the deep end."

Hopper closed his eyes for a moment, thinking, his hands clenched on the bed rails.

Tasha interjected. "You're the FBI, what do you have to worry about?"

"The place where people like Hatfield and Joe come from, well, they don't care much for following the rules. They have an unlimited budget and a great deal of moral flexibility. We're going to have to be really careful how we approach this," Sullivan said shaking his head.

Hopper made a decision and looked over at Tasha in the dim light. "He's right, we need to rethink this. It's going to take time to sort out how to proceed. In the meantime, recover... and keep your mouth shut. Understand?"

She nodded. Sullivan moved to the window to remove his jammer, and just before he did so, Tasha spoke up.

"Why are you investigating Joe?"

"Because he works outside the law. Because he doesn't fear the law."

Tasha digested that statement before responding. "He's cunning and brutal. He anticipates that you'll be better than he is. Remember he's like a wolf and they travel in packs."

Hopper looked directly into her eyes, contemplating what she'd said. A grim smile formed on his lips and he signaled Sullivan to remove the jammer. The two agents quietly exited the room, leaving Tasha in the dark, her stomach in knots about what lay ahead.

CHAPTER TEN

Three months later—8pm local time

Tasha sat in a conference room temporarily set up as a hot desk for the recent crime wave. Three women had gone missing from the area, no bodies found. No security camera footage, no ransom notes. Once again the local police department couldn't find kidnap victims, and the media was having a field day.

In the aftermath of the explosion at the farm, Tasha had gone after Samantha West and tried to tie her to Brian. They had the evidence from the party and Brian's office, but the judge had thrown out the evidence from the data server at the school due to the lack of a warrant, resulting in the case being dropped. Since then, West had been relentlessly hounding her in nightly broadcasts about the lack of progress in solving the disappearances, repeatedly explaining with each new missing person where she was at the time of the disappearance, "Just in case the police try to pin this kidnapping on me too!"

It was only made worse by the video releases from Brian claiming they would never catch him and never save the girls.

Most of the videos contained snippets of Helen during her captivity, but he had inserted clips from cab rides involving other people who were obviously not Helen but were also impossible to identify or link to the other missing person cases. This left the public assuming that the police weren't telling them about the rest of the missing girls. A great deal of the footage came from the inside of the *Zoom!* cabs. It hadn't taken long for the company to go out of business.

Theories about the disappearances ranged from a copycat killer to an accomplice never caught. Tasha had played her theory with West as far as it would go, but at most it seemed she'd helped Brian in exchange for a story. Nobody believed she had a hand in the kidnapping.

Even the FBI was stumped, blanketing high-risk areas with undercover agents, searching the rivers and lakes for any sign of a body. Even with the ongoing drought lowering the lake levels it was still taking weeks, and with each search completed there was the risk that the killer would dump the body in the lake they'd just searched.

The public was becoming impatient, and all Tasha could do was run the hot desk, waiting for leads—her punishment, evidently, for Helen's demise.

She pulled up the final report the FBI had sent her on the ranch incident and flipped through the pages, firmly clenching a stress ball in her hand ten times per page. They'd told her six months to rehab her injuries, torn ligaments and damaged tendons taking the longest.

Kyper Ranch Report Summary: Agent Casey Hopper
  Helen Knudsen Kidnapping
  Jacob Kyper and daughter Mina were discovered under the foundation of a shed in southwest corner of property. Jacob's

cause of death appears to be single gunshot wound to the head. Entry wound consistent with a gunshot from behind while standing from a person of similar height. Mina Kyper cause of death undetermined, evidence of restraints applied to ankles and wrists. No DNA linking to any known suspect.

"That's helpful," Tasha muttered. "Can't even link their deaths to our known suspect."

Lead investigator's note: Primary theory is that suspect was infatuated with Mina during their mutual time at the autonomous cab company. When she didn't respond to his advances, he reacted violently, resulting in the deaths of Mina and Jacob. Suspect was able to assume control of their finances and continue paying bills at the house.

Helen Knudsen killed by single shot through east wall of room she was held in. Round entered left ventricle causing sudden, catastrophic loss of blood and death (see autopsy report). Wound caused by an unintentional discharge from police detective Tasha Strauss's gun during struggle with the principal suspect in kitchen/dining area.

Extensive computer system on the property does not trace to any known purchases by Jacob Kyper. Several computers trace to his daughter's college use. Data was removed from the system prior to inspection. Unknown data destruction program was used. Attempted reconstruction of data and user profiles was unsuccessful.

One removable media device was located at the scene (see image 2145). Device appears to have been kicked under the couch. Device contained one terabyte of data, mostly network traffic metrics and security footage of several companies around town. Forty-one percent of all footage was of facilities owned by or supporting the conglomerate the KaliSun Initiative, aka the KSI. The KSI is a private space development firm with facilities across the United States and in the South Pacific, as well as a lunar base. The firm is primarily an American holding, with few international investors and limited government contracts. Public statements are available. Images 4532–4548 depict known employees outside KSI facilities. Suspect appeared focused on these employees, reason unknown.

Tasha pulled up the images on her tablet and swiped through them slowly. Edward Stokes, listed as CEO of KSI, and several bodyguards. A large man standing next to a woman, with the caption "Marcus Green." A series of images of an older man labeled with different captions including "The German," "The Doctor," and "WK." An FBI notation next to the last one indicated it was Walter Kapple, a geneticist at the KSI. But it was the final image that grabbed her attention.

She expanded the image on her screen, dissecting it detail by detail. It was an image pulled from a security camera showing Dr. Kapple, Steve Lavoy, and the nurse who had cared for her at the bombsite escorting a hospital gurney down a hallway. The cryptic caption drew her attention. *Unknown test subject for WK's program.*

"Kapple's program?"

Significant efforts were made by the suspect to identify individuals associated with Knudsen. All surveillance data on the drive is from the three days prior to Helen Knudsen's disappearance. It appears that most surveillance was triggered based on guests at Helen Knudsen's birthday party. No KSI employees were listed as guests on the official registry; however, image 4549 indicates that KSI employees Steve Lavoy and Walter Kapple visited with Knudsen just prior to the party for unknown reasons. The meeting appears to have drawn the suspect's interest in KSI and caused him to extensively investigate their local facilities prior to kidnapping Helen Knudsen. It is the best assessment of the investigative team that the suspect intended to kidnap Helen Knudsen, and that KSI involvement was coincidental to that act.

KSI provided investigative support to local law enforcement and Knudsen personally. They supplied all information requested immediately and in a timely manner upon request. KSI is not deemed involved in the kidnapping at this point.

"So he plans his attack, studies the layout and proceeds. He looks at the KSI intensely and dismisses them as a non-threat." Tasha snorted in derision, then muttered under her breath, "I made that mistake too. Cost you more than me."

All post-event social media messaging was accomplished through the use of prescheduled uploads. Files were stored as zero day exploits on the computers of unsuspecting users and uploaded on a predetermined timeline. Most of the footage is stock footage from foreign films. The clips were low quality and used quick cuts to prevent association with the original source. There is no evidence linking this assailant to more recent disappearances.

High probability that suspect was operating alone and has an obsession with punishing the rich. See forensic psychology report at below hyperlink for motives and aggravating factors.

The phone rang, interrupting her before she could click on the hyperlink.

"Missing persons, Detective Tasha Strauss speaking."

"Missing persons? I uh, I guess that works. This is the Mendoza trauma ward. We have a female, age about twenty-four, who is claiming she was abducted four days ago. She's not very coherent right now, but I think we need somebody to come take a statement from her. She has a high fever and is not very stable. Can you—"

"I'm on my way, don't let anyone else see her or talk to her." Tasha leaped out of her chair and raced down the hallway, dialing a number into her cell as she went.

The phone rang three times before Agent Hopper answered, sounding distracted.

"Hopper, meet me down at Mendoza trauma ward immediately, we've got a girl down there claiming she was abducted. I'm on my way now."

Hopper stuttered a response before acknowledging that he would be there as soon as possible.

Tasha winced when she pushed the door violently with her bad arm, then jogged to her car and peeled out of the parking lot.

The head nurse was waiting for her at the doors of the emergency room, an anxious look on her face. Once inside, Tasha strode deeper into the building, following the nurse and urging her on faster.

"Ok, tell me what you know."

"A trail runner was taking his morning route along the Sipercino Trail early this morning. A flash of color at the base of the ravine caught his attention and he investigated. He couldn't get down the hill, but he was able to get close enough to see it was a woman, so he called the sheriff and they brought her here. She—"

"Wait, you found her at *what time* this morning and you're only just telling us now?" Tasha rolled her eyes in agony as she pushed another door out of the way.

"She only got to us two hours ago, it took a while to get her out of the ravine. I guess it's very steep." The nurse took a deep breath before continuing. "Initially we thought she'd slipped down the trail and suffered broken bones and possibly a concussion, because she was saying things that didn't make sense. So we ran some x-rays and did some preliminary tests." The nurse turned sharply and hit an elevator call button.

"I thought you said she was in the ER?"

"One of your people called and asked us to move her up to observation for now."

"One of my people? Who?"

The nurse shrugged as she walked into the elevator and punched the button for the third floor. "We were thinking she had a some kind of virus, but as more tests came back, it became clear there's something else going on."

Tasha stepped out of the elevator, following the nurse down the hall. "It's like her DNA is being attacked by some kind of solvent almost. There's soft tissue degeneration across most of her major organs."

"Like Ebola or something?" Tasha said, nearly skidding to a halt in alarm.

"We thought so at first, entered into contamination protocol, but we called in an expert in immunology, and they confirmed that whatever it is, it can't be transmitted except through bodily fluids. So she's safe, we just aren't sure of a treatment protocol yet."

They arrived at a door near a freight elevator at the end of the hallway and the nurse gestured her in. "I'm not sure how much she can help. She has a high fever and it's causing her some cognition problems. Good luck detective."

Tasha entered the room cautiously. The woman's athletic body was wracked with unproductive coughing, her skin an angry red from the fever. As Tasha approached, the girl slipped into a fitful sleep. A monitor showed her fever hovering around 103 degrees.

Tasha paused and turned to the chair in the corner. With a heavy sigh she settled in and began writing notes on her conversation with the nurse. She was just putting the notebook away when she realized that she didn't know the victim's name.

She peered down at the monitor. "Amy Weaver, what have you gotten yourself into?"

The door opened behind her with a soft creak. She glanced casually over her shoulder as a man in a doctor's jacket backed into the room, carefully shutting the door behind him.

"Do you have time for a couple of questions, doc?"

The doctor spun around, his eyes wide and the bald spot in the middle of his head fast turning red. He held a full syringe in his hand. Tasha looked curiously at the unexpected reaction—then it hit her. She knew this man. He was one of Knudsen's bodyguards.

"Elliot? Wha... what are you doing here?" she stammered as her hand dropped to her weapon and she tried to back up.

He lunged forward and tried to pin her to the chair, knocking her gun away. The syringe was still capped, but he tried to jab her with it anyway, forcing his weight down on her bad arm as he drove his knee up into her thigh. She coughed hard and her arm gave way, letting his fist through to smash into her face with a sickening thud.

She lay in a daze on the floor. He stood over her, a condescending smile forming on his lips. He pulled the cap off the needle. Tasha's head lolled to the side as she tried to scoot away across the floor, searching for her weapon. He nudged a toe under her hip, preparing to flip her onto her stomach and inject her, when a noise from the door caused him to pause and turn his head.

A second man, dressed in blue scrubs and a surgical mask, entered the room and delivered a swift kick to the back of Elliot's knee. He dropped the syringe, falling to the ground in pain. The man followed up with a chop to the neck, then cupped his hands and savagely beat them down on Elliot's eardrums. Grunting weakly, Elliot started to tumble forward, but the man reached down and caught him by his thinning hair, stopping his fall. The man reached around to pull Elliot's tie, roughly tightened the knot at his throat, and gripped the tie as he pushed him forward.

The tie crushed Elliot's throat. Spit and blood flew onto Tasha's shirt as Elliot hung suspended over her. The man pushed Elliot's head forward and pulled the tie back, breathing heavily through his mask. Elliot's eyes bulged, only relaxing as the life drained from his body. The capillaries in his right eye burst and the man in blue scrubs dropped him with a thud on the ground.

The second doctor squatted in front of Tasha, reaching a latex glove down to check her pulse. Her vision focused on him for a second, noticing the calm, steady breathing through the mask and the intense look in his eyes. She squinted at him through the blood in her eyes.

"Joe?"

The man grunted softly and stood up, opening the door again and checking the hallway. He disappeared for a moment, then returned, pushing a wheelchair into the room. He picked Amy up off the bed, wrapping the sheets from her bed around her, and placed her gently in the chair. He set her pillow in her lap, then sprayed an unmarked liquid where her head, back, and butt had sweated through the sheets. Wisps of acrid smoke rose off the bed as the liquid soaked in. He wiped down the rails with a rag that smelled strongly of bleach then tossed the rag into a bag hanging off the back of the wheelchair. He carefully detached the woman's IVs from the monitor system, hooked them to her chair, and disarmed the monitor alarms. Without looking again at Tasha, he wheeled the sick woman across the hall into the waiting freight elevator.

Tasha tried to push Elliot's dead weight off her, but the struggle had reinjured the ligaments in her arm, and she couldn't budge him. Her phone lay on the floor nearby, shattered by the impact with the chair she'd been slammed into. After several attempts to use the phone, she gave up, relaxing back on the floor and taking several deep breaths before yelling for help.

The ER doctor finished his examination of Tasha in the hall outside Amy's room, handing her off to the nurse as the argument between the mayor and Captain Jackson continued next to her. The nurse had Tasha tilt her head back, stitching the area above her eye where Elliot had punched her. She moved quickly and with ease, dabbing the area with gauze and antiseptic.

"Nineteen stitches. His ring got you good."

"Yeah."

"Well, all done. You'll need to schedule the MRI the doctor ordered before you leave tonight," the nurse said as she stripped off her gloves and collected the rest of her things.

Tasha took a deep breath and stood up, touching her face

gingerly. The motion caused the argument to falter as the three men turned to face her.

"I understand you're upset. I got to her as fast as I could. Before I was able to question her I was attacked and—"

"And you, a trained police detective, lost to a man with a needle. You lost and now another girl is gone. At some point it might be time to recognize you aren't cut out for this," the mayor said incredulously.

"I'm still recovering from the last fight I was in. They say another three months at the minim—"

"Another a fight you shouldn't have lost. You had your weapon out and you got beat by somebody you had the drop on."

"A serial killer—" the captain tried to interject.

"He wasn't a serial killer," the mayor corrected. "He was a nerd who preyed on the weak, abusing a automated cab technology that should never have been allowed in the first place. Now I have a police department that can't figure out how young women are disappearing from right under their noses. Tell me why I should keep you, Jackson? Tell me why I should tolerate your lack of... competence. Tell me."

"Removing me won't get you closer to solving this problem. Removing me or my people will just take away any continuity the investigation has at this point. Even the FBI can't figure out how these girls are being taken or what's happening to them. With no crime scene, no bodies, no trail of any kind, it's hard to make progress."

"You had a victim, a living victim effectively in police custody, the key to this entire case and somehow you lost her. In a damn hospital." The mayor leaned in close, looking up at him and poking his chest hard. "Fix this, *now*."

The mayor turned and stalked out, his driver and aide running to catch up.

Jackson waited for the mayor to move out of earshot and the medical staff to clear out before grabbing Tasha by her good arm and pulling her away from the crime scene investigators. He looked down into her eyes, his hand still gripping her arm tightly.

"I need to know what happened. All of it."

"That's Knudsen's thug on the floor in there," Tasha said with a slight nod toward the corpse barely visible through the cracked door. "As you've guessed, I didn't kill him. Somebody had Amy moved up here by the freight elevator. Not sure if it was Elliot or..." She took a deep breath, gazing steadily at her captain's face. "Joe."

The skin around Jackson's eyes and mouth tightened, and he glared into the hospital room.

"Are you sure it was him? Elliot landed a pretty heavy shot to your head." He paused, a frown on his face. "This would be the third time you've thought he was part of the equation, and the previous two times it didn't pan out. We need to be sure."

"He had a mask on, but I'm pretty sure. Elliot isn't a small man, and the man who killed him just broke him. It was almost... *routine*, like doing chores. I bet when they process that scene there isn't a fingerprint, a stray piece of hair, or a piece of fabric we can link to a third person in that fight."

"No security camera footage either. IT department says they had a malfunction in the cameras and lost the data," Jackson admitted grudgingly. "Elliot might have managed that without Joe, though. It's not like their system was top of the line."

"Yeah, I worked with Joe for a couple of days. He's a professional. It was him."

The lead lab technician walked out of Amy's room and approached them. "I've got fingerprints from eleven people in there. It's going to take a while to sort it out. Two blood types, assuming one is the detective's. Fair bit of aspirated blood on the walls and floor. I'm assuming it's a mix of the victim's and the detective's..."

"The assailant," Tasha corrected him. "He was the aggressor."

"Ok, noted. The girl is gone. Whoever took her took the sheets and every piece of medical equipment that had her DNA on it. The mattress under the sheets was also sprayed with a pretty strong acid, we can't pull anything out of that mess."

"You shouldn't need her DNA, the hospital has a record of who she is and her medical records. Finding her again shouldn't be a problem..." Tasha's voice trailed off when she saw the tech's face. "What?"

"Her files are gone off the mainframe and the backup. Also, the tissue and blood samples they sent to the lab are gone. Do you want my opinion?"

Tasha sighed and waved him on.

"We're in the deep end, swimming with the sharks."

"What did you just say?" Tasha said with sudden interest.

"Deep end? Of the pool?" the tech responded with a questioning look.

The captain looked at her with a frown. "Anything else?" he prodded the tech.

"We'll know more tomorrow or the next day. I assume this is top priority in the lab?"

"Yes, keep hard copies and post two extra guards around the evidence lockup at all times."

"Sure, overtime authorized?"

"Yes, just don't lose what little evidence we have. We've got enough problems right now."

The tech nodded and walked away, leaving them alone in the hallway.

"Try other security systems around the area, maybe we can get a glimpse of a vehicle leaving. I'll deal with the FBI."

"We need to get eyes on all of Knudsen's people, and after that," Tasha jerked her head toward Elliot's corpse, "I want a warrant to raid Knudsen's place."

Jackson sighed deeply. "Elliot didn't live on the premises did he?"

"No, an apartment in Valdez if I remember."

"So his body really only gives us airtight probable cause to search that, which we will. We need more to get to Knudsen. Start digging."

"If Knudsen is behind the abductions, Elliot's death could make him change his behavior. Catching him in the act would be tough," Tasha pointed out.

"Try to be subtle."

Tasha pointed at her recent stitches. The captain nodded and looking up at the hallway surveillance camera, deep in thought.

CHAPTER ELEVEN

Steve Lavoy started the engine and pulled out onto the coastal highway, merging seamlessly into traffic, the dark sedan humming as he accelerated.

"Drone is on station and tracking, push up two klicks." Joe was in the back seat watching the drone footage on a flexible screen clipped to the back of the front passenger seat. In his lap he cradled a compact, non-visible laser, the kind typically used for industrial cutting. Joe had it modified with modular rifle parts so he could fire it out of the window.

Lavoy maneuvered through traffic, steadily gaining on the target vehicle. "First window of opportunity is in about four klicks, you ready back there?"

"Yeah. At fifty meters from the target, roll the window down, I'll try for the back right tire."

Lavoy nodded, making another pass and pressing a button on the display. A map with police symbols scattered across it appeared on the center console. "Looks like we have a pretty decent window, probable police response time to first kill zone is about eleven minutes. No surveillance systems for about three miles. This part of the highway is pretty clean. Next kill zone isn't, so first chance is our best chance."

"Noted." Joe was silent for a long moment. "When you confronted Knudsen, what did he say?"

"I told him he was violating the agreement we had, endangering himself and our interests—not to mention the women he's killing. He started yelling about how he'd already lost so much, that we needed to indulge him. He demanded we find him a girl he couldn't infect. I told him the gene patterns would have to be so close she would almost have to be related to him and that we wanted no part in that. Guy loses his shit, has this knucklehead ahead of us point a gun at me. Tells me not to come back or else he'll tell the police everything."

"So are we bagging this guy because he pointed a gun at you or because of the threat to the company?"

"Stokes called it in. He thinks the only way to curtail this is to take away the people who are getting him the girls. If we do that, either he stops or he gets sloppy. If the cops grab him, we'll move on to other options."

"And if the feds get him?"

"We've got the feds covered, we'll know about that in plenty of time to act."

Joe grunted, shifting the laser up onto the seat in front of him, the headrest blocking anyone from seeing the gun through the windshield.

"Any idea how he's picking the girls?"

"Yeah he told me—apparently they found some quack scientist that gave them a tool that compares pictures of his daughter to people he sees on dating sites. If the software thinks they share enough genetic markers, it flags them. So Elliot used the tool to scope out prospective girlfriends for his boss on fling dating sites and he'd pick 'em up. When didn't go well, the girl would disappear. With Elliot dead, we're not likely to find the bodies any time soon. Just another mess we need to be ready to clean up when somebody stumbles across them."

"Glad to see the scientific method is alive and well. You'd think a researcher would know that was a stupid way to get around the rules."

"Knudsen's not a medical researcher, he's a wave form nerd. Not all scientists are created equal," Lavoy said with a sarcastic laugh.

"Did you already take care of the guy who gave him the software?"

"Didn't have to. Our friend up ahead tracked him down and caved in his skull with a baseball bat when Elliot died. I guess he blamed him."

"Probably left a boatload of evidence too," Joe scoffed. "Actually, that might come in handy later if the FBI gets that far."

"Target in sight. Just went around a bend, about two hundred meters."

The car accelerated slightly, the electric engine whisper-quiet as they moved into position. The front passenger window dropped, filling the car with gusting wind. Lavoy lowered the back seat window an inch, letting the air flow out of the cabin.

"Target in range, make sure you don't hit the mirror," he said as he scanned the traffic for anyone paying attention.

"Yeah, got it. I've got the illuminator on the wheel, give me a count until the curve," Joe said, watching the targeting reticle intently.

"Stand by," Lavoy said. The two cars followed the curve in the road and he held the sedan locked in a following position. "Ready... Steady... 5... 4... 3... 2... 1, light him up."

"Firing." The laser made a soft beep, the strong smell of ozone filling the car briefly before being whipped out the back window.

Ahead of them, the target vehicle tracked around the curve smoothly before a flare of light burned through the rubber on the back right tire. The tire immediately blew out, dropping the rim to the pavement in a shower of sparks. The car fish-tailed hard as the back end swung wide, spraying gravel. The driver lost control in an attempt to whip back the other way, catching the tires and flipping the car into a barrel roll.

Debris flew in all directions as the top of the car crumpled in and the wreck tumbled across the median, sideswiping an oncoming truck and launching into the top of the guardrail before sailing over the edge of the cliff. It tumbled erratically down the hill and landed with a splash in the ocean below.

Lavoy rolled the windows up nearly to the top, letting the thin opening pull the ozone smell out of the car. Joe turned the laser off and set it down, then hooked the drone control box to the seat in front of him.

"Nice shot, how's it looking?" Lavoy asked, focused on leaving the scene without drawing attention.

"Damn electric cars don't explode like the old gas ones would."

"Did it make the water? Maybe we'll get lucky and he'll drown."

Joe moved the drone out over the ocean, carefully positioning it so anyone looking on from the shore would have the sun in their eyes. He watched as thin tendrils of smoke and steam rose from the crashed car.

"It's in the water, looks like we have three cars and a truck involved with the accident on the highway. Some debris strikes on the cars, the truck appears to have clipped the wreck pretty hard."

"No autonomous vehicles?"

"I don't see a driver getting out of the truck, either he's injured or it's a bot truck."

"Company?"

"Peking Express, written in English and one of the Chinese languages." Joe paused, changing the camera angle. "Damn, I've got movement by the wreck. He's trying to exit the rear of the vehicle."

"Tough bastard," Lavoy said with a sigh. He grabbed the encrypted phone from the center console and dialed a number. A female answered the phone. "Need to place an order for some Chinese food, Peking Express. Sweet'n'sour, make sure you wipe the sauce off. I don't need a receipt. Thanks sweetie!"

Lavoy hung up the phone and put it back in the center console. "Dana is working on getting any video feeds from that truck, she'll have it wiped or corrupted shortly."

"Yes," Joe said with a smile. "I've seen her work before."

Lavoy gave him a half smile in the rearview mirror and set the cruise control at five miles per hour over the limit.

"He's almost out, about half his body through the window. Vehicle's in shallow water, but the waves are giving him some trouble."

"That was a textbook move. Hard to believe he survived it," Lavoy said in disbelief.

Joe was silent, maneuvering the drone for a better angle. "I see some smoke, looks like it's from under the center of the car."

"Is the car upside down?"

"Yes, looks like the... whoa. Vehicle just went boom."

"What? What do you mean?"

"It's in pieces. Fireball just caught the whole damn hill on fire. The battery pack must have blown."

"Salt water and a lithium ion battery, should have seen that coming. Did he survive the explosion?"

"I don't see him, I can't see how he'd make it out of that. I'm clearing the drone out. Head on back to the barn."

CHAPTER TWELVE

"Detective, take a look at this." The CSI tech held up a binder for inspection.

Tasha adjusted her gloves and took the binder. Inside she found several pages of names with associated phone numbers and email addresses, and some overseas bank account numbers. Her eyes narrowed as she scanned the phone numbers, and she pulled her phone out for a quick internet search.

Jackson walked into the room and stood next to her, looking at the binder.

"There are no signs of anyone being held against their will here, a woman's curling iron and a few hair brushes in the bathroom, nothing really that interesting. Did you find something?"

"Maybe. This binder has a bunch of contacts in it, some bank accounts. There aren't any values for how much is in the accounts, but the phone numbers and internet domains are interesting. About half of the list uses country code extensions that indicate Costa Rica and Panama. Then we have another group of phone numbers for South America, but all of the bank account numbers seem to be associated with those two countries."

"Maybe Elliot was planning a trip."

"I suppose it's possible," Tasha said with a vague wave at the wall art depicting combat scenes and half naked women. "Although he doesn't seem like the environmental tourist kind of guy.

Tasha shook her head, studying the binder, trying to find the thread tying recent events and the evidence in the apartment into a coherent story. The contacts were coded with small hand-sketched drawings—several huts, a palm tree with a sun next to it, a boat, and a poor depiction of the mud-flap girl.

"The only common theme between any of the victims that we found was that they were young and active on discrete hook-up dating services. But they didn't all use the same service and they weren't all from the same area."

"Pretty thin connection," Jackson said.

"Well, ignore everything we know about the kidnappings for a moment. Just pretend we have no prior history with Elliot. A girl is found at the bottom of a hillside, gravely ill and claiming she was kidnapped. She is taken to the hospital and Elliot shows up and tries to kill her. Joe kills Elliot and takes our victim away, and afterwards all evidence of her medical data is gone, stripped to nothing by somebody talented. What connections do we have between Joe and Elliot?"

"Knudsen," Jackson said through clenched teeth.

"And we know that whoever can wipe out hospital records and remove the test samples without a trace is skilled and probably has a lot of resources. Points to Joe's employer. The KSI was helping Knudsen when his daughter vanished, but one of their employees killed Knudsen's man in the hospital. Now, it always seemed strange that the KSI would help Knudsen out of the goodness of their hearts, so I assumed it was a business relationship. But it seems they've had a falling out. This feels like a cover up, which would mean that since they already got Elliot they may move on to Knudsen next."

"If Joe was at the hospital for Elliot and not the girl, why did he take the girl? Didn't Knudsen have another aide or body guard besides Elliot?"

"Yes, Micah Crastin."

"What do we know about his activities lately?"

"I've had Detective Berntino keeping track of him since the hospital incident. Nothing to spook him, nothing too close, just following him and watching his credit card usage. I'd rather go after a search warrant for Knudsen's place. He feels dirty as hell—anything that causes people to go to this much trouble is worth looking into."

"I talked to Agent Hopper about that, he feels that our evidence on Knudsen's involvement is pretty weak. Wanted us to wait until we'd processed this place, see if we could tighten up the probable cause. Seems he feels like Knudsen's going to have some pretty good legal coverage."

Tasha hefted the binder at Jackson. "Like you said, looks like he was planning a trip. Some South American countries don't have extradition."

Jackson's next comment was cut off by Tasha's phone ringing. She checked the display with a frown and answered it. The person on the other end spoke loudly, with a great deal of wind noise in the background, and Tasha had to hold the phone away from her ear. She listened intently, told the person to send her an emailed summary, and hung up.

"That was Berntino. Crastin is dead, he had a massive blowout on the coastal highway and his car hit a truck before going off a cliff. Battery exploded. Right now they have fire rescue trying to get to the crash site, but the entire hillside ignited, and the flames jumped up onto the highway. He says eleven cars and a couple of trucks were caught in the flames and now the fire's headed over the ridge toward a residential area. It's uncontained and spreading rapidly."

Jackson stared at her, slowly shaking his head. "No, no, that's too convenient. Search warrant for Knudsen's house now. You get the papers straight, I'll get a judge."

Tasha grinned. "I wrote it last night when I wrote out the justification for the apartment."

"Update it with whatever you can from here. We'll also push on the judge that we believe Knudsen's life might be in danger and that our search is to confirm he's safe. It might be flimsy in court, but it gets us in the door!"

Tasha stood in almost the same spot where she'd first met Martin Knudsen. Papers were strewn everywhere, the desk had been ransacked, and in thirty minutes they hadn't found a single functioning electronic device of any kind. Even the electronics in the smart appliances had been ripped out, the remaining solid-state components fried into grease by high voltage. A crime scene tech came into the room looking discouraged and handed her a tablet.

"Security system is gone, backup is gone. Somebody went through this house and dismantled or destroyed everything that could have a memory. Internet voice recognition is toast, the receivers and CPU were dismantled, memory is gone and the remaining components were burned in an incinerator out back. They even prevented the breakers from tripping and ran a surge through the house to fry anything they missed. This guy's people are pros, I've never seen a house sent back to the Stone Age like this."

Jackson entered the room and walked dejectedly over to where Tasha stood, papers scuttling across his path in the breeze from the open courtyard window.

"This is bullshit," Tasha said. "We delayed, and now not only is Knudsen gone, but the digital fingerprint in this house has been eradicated."

"I'm sorry."

"The tech thinks Knudsen's people did it."

"Yeah, we talked already."

"You know it was the KSI. This has Joe written all over it."

Jackson let out a heavy sigh. "It sure seems that way. Do you want the other bad news?"

Tasha slowly turned her head, eyes narrowed. "What?"

"Knudsen Advanced Research was hit by a cyber attack this morning. The FBI is being tight-lipped about it, but early indicators seem to point towards a state-sponsored attack. It looks like a rip, burn, and run. I think the only reason the feds told us is because we showed up with a warrant while they were onsite."

"Don't tell me by burn you mean..."

"Their entire email system and backups were stolen and then purged. Their offsite data storage backup was also hit."

"Just their email?"

"Yes, they had their research material on an isolated network. That seems to be secure, although the FBI cyber response team is out there investigating to see if they can spot any intrusions or exfiltration."

"So we're *on the way* with a warrant to search their email and they get wiped."

"Yes," Jackson said flatly, his face settling into a grimace.

"Detective?" A CSI tech called to Tasha from across the room. "Better take a look at this."

They walked over to the tech, who was kneeling on the floor fingering three neat holes drilled into the floor. A partially unpacked box sat on the floor next to him, next to a drill.

"You told me to x-ray the walls and look for anything hidden. It took a while for the box to get here, and when I went to set it up I noticed this."

"What am I looking at?" Tasha asked.

"This is where we'd set the machine up to scan the room. The procedure is to place it on the floor, attach it with the drill, and drop this sensor rod down to the floor. It sends out a combination of x-rays and vibrations through the building, then the image processor combines them and produces the scan."

"And?"

"We're the first crew in here. This is brand new technology; we had to send away to the State CID to borrow it. The holes in the floor aren't from me. Somebody already used a machine, like this one, to scan the room. Very recently."

"Screw it, scan the room anyway. I'm sick of this crap," Tasha said, stalking into the hallway. Jackson followed.

"I was thinking," Jackson said. "The timeline doesn't work. How far away was Crastin when he died?"

"An hour, maybe ninety minutes in traffic. Why?"

"Assume that wasn't an accident, there is no way Joe was involved in that, then made it back here and stripped this place this completely in the three hours it took us to get the warrant approved. Especially since we had a patrol car watching the place inside of fifteen minutes of the call."

"Berntino didn't get to the accident scene right away."

"What?"

"He thought following him would be too obvious with how small that highway is. He overheard Crastin tell somebody he was going to the parking garage near the El Dorado taco bar, so he drove there first and waited. It wasn't until he heard there was a fire on the scanner that he thought to check the position of Crastin's car."

"He had a tracker on it?"

"Yeah, don't worry. It wasn't department issued."

Jackson raised an eyebrow.

"So they had a four hour window, give or take, before the patrol unit showed."

"Four hours. It doesn't seem possible," Jackson said under his breath.

"Probably had that asshole Lavoy helping him."

"Detective, scan is complete. We've found a wall safe and a concealed firearm," the tech called excitedly from the other room.

They walked back to Knudsen's desk, watching as the tech carefully examined the bookshelf behind the desk. He tried several books, tugging on them and pushing them back in without success before he grabbed the shelf itself and pulled on it. With a click the wall opened up, exposing an impressive safe. As the hidden panel cleared the hinges, the safe door came ajar, a large blackened hole marked where the tumbler had been. The tech pulled the safe door open the rest of the way and peered in.

Scraps of paper slipped out, but all that remained was a small stack of hundreds and a framed picture of Martin Knudsen and Helen together on an empty beach. The felt lining inside the safe was depressed where numerous objects had formerly rested.

Tasha rubbed her face slowly, frustrated. "Check the picture frame, make sure he didn't hide anything in there."

The tech took several photos before carefully extracting the frame and examining it on the desk.

"Standard frame, simple picture. No hidden data disk if that's what you were hoping for, Detective."

"What's that lettering on the back?" Captain Jackson asked, gesturing at the back corner.

"It says, 'Pura Vida! Puerto Jiménez, Costa Rica.'"

Jackson gave Tasha a pained look, and she nodded in agreement before turning back to the tech.

"And the gun?"

"It's concealed in his desk chair. If you pull the lever to lower the chair and twist at the same time, it pops out the back of the chair. Large caliber Glock with a spare mag."

"Illegal in this state for years, if we ever manage to find him again," Jackson said.

"Yeah," Tasha said absently. She turned to the tech. "Continue your search. Also, I want every scrap of paper accounted for. Send the serial numbers on the bills in the safe to Treasury and see if they have anything to say." She looked back to Jackson. "They can't have gotten everything, nobody is perfect."

"Knudsen's gone, Tasha. Flown the coop or buried in a field somewhere."

They left the techs to finish up, walking quietly through the abandoned mansion. With a complex this large, they'd pulled in crime scene teams from three other local departments, and it was still going to be a weekend-long investigation if they were lucky.

"One last place to check for him."

Jackson turned and gave her a penetrating look, before glancing behind her into the office they had just vacated.

"I can't authorize you to operate outside our jurisdiction, never mind in another country."

"I've had a lot of stress lately, maybe I need a vacation," Tasha said evenly.

"And if you find him, then what? I'm not sure you've thought this through." He took a deep breath. "If you're dead set on chasing him, at least let the FBI know so they can do the arresting if you find him."

"Let's see if I can find him first."

CHAPTER THIRTEEN

Tasha sat huddled under the overhang of a small café, cradling a cup of coffee and watching the rain pour down. She was feeling stiff and a little unsettled by the bumpy landing earlier that morning. A shudder ran down her spine as she remembered the small prop plane careening through the rainstorm and landing on the narrow runway in Puerto Jiménez. The jungle had whipped by the windows, before the plane screeched to a halt near the cemetery where she and the other passengers disembarked.

Darkness was falling and she still needed a place to stay, but the main street in town didn't look promising. The road was crumbling away, regular heavy rains having eroded the asphalt and left huge potholes now filled with muddy water. Mosquitoes formed a haze over the hood of her raincoat.

The locals scarcely seemed to notice her, or the rain for that matter, walking calmly down the sidewalks, chatting and laughing—not an umbrella in sight. Dirt bikes wound their way around the potholes and cars. She pulled out her book on Costa Rica and stared at the map. Jackson had given her permission to come, but no money and very little intel, just the airport tourist guide and a ten-minute lecture on not getting crossways with the local police. She flipped to a description of the area.

Puerto Jiménez is located at the southern end of the Osa Peninsula, in the southwestern section of Puntarenas. The harbor provides access to the Golfo Dulce, a deep-water marine life sanctuary that is home to large populations of sea turtles and whales. Access to local roadways is available, allowing travel to Cabo Matapalo, Carate, and Rincon. The airport is convenient to the town center and provides transportation to San Jose, Golfito, and seasonal flights to Northern Costa Rica. A water taxi is also available to Golfito across the Golfo, a common route to Panama, just to the south. Golfo Dulce is fed by numerous rivers through extensive mangrove swamps, hosting an incredibly diverse array of wild life including Dolphins and Salt Water Crocodiles. Golfo Dulce exits into the Pacific Ocean near Cabo Matapolo.

Tasha sighed, swatting at her face to fend off the mosquitoes, and leaned back heavily in her chair, causing it to creak ominously. A waitress wandered out toward her, coffee pot in hand.

"Hola."

"Hola, como esta? Habla English?"

"Yes, I speak a little inglés."

"I'm looking for a place to stay. Can you help?"

The waitress looked at Tasha's wet luggage piled up against the wall, and smiled.

"You have a car?"

"No, not yet."

"It's ok. My friend can drive you. There are many places to

stay. You want an eco-tour lodge, experience the wilds of Costa Rica?"

In the distance a spider monkey called loudly, a pair of scarlet macaws flew over and settled in the tree near the grocery store, and a beat up SUV rumbled up the street, spraying muddy water in great arcs toward the sidewalk. Tasha looked up at the waitress and smiled tiredly.

"Something on the cheaper side, with air conditioning and WiFi. Do you have WiFi down here?"

"Of course." The waitress smiled, turning the napkin dispenser toward her so she could see the side that had the connection information and an ad for a local fisherman. "I know a place close to the beach. Not too expensive now. I will call and ask if they have room if you want?"

"Thank you, that's very helpful."

"Con mucho gusto!"

The waitress bustled off, dialing on her phone. Tasha stared out at the muddy street. A couple of teenagers rode past on dirt bikes, one clutching a soccer ball, and a police truck slowly crept along the street. A man stepped off the porch of the restaurant across the street and flagged down the cop car. The truck pulled up and a friendly conversation ensued.

She watched the meet-up idly, professional curiosity about another country's police force drawing her attention. Nice truck, not heavily used. The lack of tactical accessories was a significant departure from the trucks in her department. When the conversation died down, the truck pulled away and the man waved and cut across the street, heading toward the café where Tasha sat. He walked with his head down, rain sleeting off his hat and raincoat, only looking up at the last moment before he stepped onto the sidewalk and veered up the street toward one of the small bars.

Tasha's breath caught in her throat—it was Agent Hopper.

Dressed like a tourist, but definitely him, his angular face and gray eyes a marked contrast to the locals. He did not appear to notice her, but walked briskly, eyes down, skirting around mud puddles.

An SUV rumbled up the street and stopped in front of the café, and a young Costa Rican waved cheerfully at her from the window. Tasha hesitated, torn between following Hopper and getting a ride... and a bed. She realized that leaving her gear at the restaurant might garner some unwanted attention so she grabbed it and threw it in the back seat of the SUV before climbing into the front seat. She tried to roll the window up to keep out the rain, but the driver laughed and shook his head no.

She tried to talk to him, but he shook his head again and held up a handwritten note with the price to get her to the hotel. She did some mental math and shrugged—tourist prices.

The car lurched down to the edge of the harbor, slipping in and out of potholes, jarring her around inside the cab. They passed several small restaurants along the brief waterfront; he paused at one and pointed at it.

"Soda," he said making eating motions. "Like café, muy bueno."

She nodded, noting the restaurant's outdoor seating and walls were covered with small lizards and bugs. Her stomach growled impatiently and the driver took off again down the street, and in several blocked pulled up to a bright blue single-level building right on the edge of a small bay. She stepped out of the vehicle into a massive mud puddle. The driver collected her bags and started into the building.

She paid for a week and found her room. Dropping her bags, she stood and looked around—single bed with a simple dresser next to it, private bathroom, two lights. The walls were brightly painted and had been adorned with pictures related to the history of the area and a couple maps from different time periods.

She rummaged through her bags, pulling out some local currency and a tablet. Stuffing the money and tablet into her inside raincoat pocket, she headed back out into the night in search of food.

Four days wandering the town looking for evidence of Knudsen had gotten her nowhere. She'd even taken the water taxi across the bay to Golfito and asked around at the dive bars, but the story was the same. Nobody had seen him, nobody had any suggestions where to look for him. So it was Tasha found herself sitting on a pier as a cruise ship pulled into port, hoping Knudsen'd either get off the ship or try to get on.

The ship took its time settling into anchorage, a host of small water taxis hovering nearby. A couple sat down near her, using binoculars to scan the boats and looking rather anxious.

"Do you see him? Is the doctor with him?" the woman asked in a thick British accent.

"Yes, blue boat, third in line," her companion answered.

Their body language made it plain that the doctor's visit wasn't for anything trivial. Thinking back to her briefings on the various diseases that the bugs carried, she decided to interject.

"Excuse me, did you say you were waiting on a doctor?"

The man started, seeming to notice her for the first time. He turned to the woman next to him, a worried look on his face, before turning back to Tasha.

"Yes, one of our marine biology students is very sick. We can't figure out why."

"What were they studying?"

"Sea turtles, hawksbill and green turtles. This is a major habitat for them, with many birthing beaches."

"Did she pick something up from the turtles?" Tasha asked with surprise.

"No, no. She said she went into town to do a monkey tour up the coast, met up with some people who gave her a ride to Matapalo. She was out there a couple of nights and came back to work. Two days ago, she got sick out of the blue. The local doctors haven't been able to figure out what the problem is," the man replied. "The worst she could catch from a sea turtle is a bout of salmonella, whatever is wrong with her is definitely not that."

"If you try to move her, or lift her up she bruises almost immediately, its like her body is deteriorating right before our eyes. Her lymph nodes are badly swollen and she's... crying blood." The woman said sadly. "She's so young, barely twenty-two. It's devastating."

"The doctors think we shouldn't try to transport her, they don't know what the pressure change will do to her body if we try to fly her out, and the roads are far too bumpy. The cruise ship doctor is her only hope unless one of the aid agencies we reached out to can fly down here."

Tasha digested what they were saying. "Did she talk about what she did in Matapalo? Who she spent time with?"

"Nothing really, she said a young guy took her out there with another couple. When they got there, he introduced her to his father and together they went on a monkey tour with one of the locals. I gather she ended up spending an extra night there, she said he was nice. Then she came back."

"She said he was rich, not that he was nice," the woman corrected him.

"Yes, yes. Some kind of fancy scientist or engineer close to retirement," he replied.

"Do you pay your researchers?" Tasha asked abruptly.

"What? Why do you ask?"

"Just curious," Tasha said, thinking quickly. "I mean, I wondered if you provide health insurance?"

"Oh, no. They have student insurance through their school. The position is unpaid, but they earn value through the experience of working on our project," the man explained proudly.

Tasha bit the inside her lip, in a week of zero leads, this was the closest she had to one—a young girl with similar symptoms to the victim in her last case, doctors can't figure it out, and tied in with a rich man that a young, broke researcher might have hooked up with for the right compensation. She reached down into her bag and pulled out her tablet.

"I'm actually looking for my friend's dad. He's staying down here with my brother, but my reception has been terrible and I can't seem to find him. But the man she met with sounds a lot like him. I don't suppose she described him at all? I have some pictures." Tasha held up a digital picture of Knudsen and Helen they had taken from the safe. "That's my friend there, and that's her dad," Tasha said, her gut tightening.

"Oh, sure, that could be him. She did have a picture she took of him, the lighting was poor and he wasn't looking at her, but she showed it to me briefly. An older man, very friendly she said," the man replied distractedly. Motion out by the cruise ship had caught his attention. He raised the binoculars again to scan the boats, his lips pressed tightly together.

"Are they coming?"

"Yes. They're on their way into the harbor." He turned to Tasha. "Good luck finding your friend. Hopefully he doesn't catch what our girl did. Wear your bug spray for sure, just to be safe."

The two researchers stood up and gave her a little wave, before crowding to the end of the dock to wait for the boat.

"I'm not sure bug spray is going to save anybody," Tasha said under her breath.

She got up and made her way to the far end of the pier where the local cab drivers waited for passengers from the cruise ship.

The SUV finally came to a bumpy stop next to a small bus shelter. Tasha clambered out, rubbing her back. She paid the driver, who waved cheerfully before doing a sloppy U-turn and zigzagging back down the hill to avoid the ruts and small rivers of rain.

The jungle choked the narrow dirt road, blocking the mid-afternoon light and trapping the heat beneath the leaves. Rain dripped steadily from the canopy above her head, and the humidity hovered thick above the ground. Tasha's clothes clung to her skin.

She wandered over to the shelter and took a seat on the damp wood, putting her day bag on the table and stretching her legs. The ride from Puerto Jiménez had been miserable. The driver hadn't gone very fast, but the road was riddled with potholes and the shocks on the truck were far past worn out. He'd done his best to dodge the worst of them, but every few minutes one would escape his attention and hammer the frame of the SUV into the ground with a jarring crash.

Twice they'd come to a spot where the road was washed out, river water freely flowing across it, and each time he'd carefully made his way through the water while she clung to the door frame, praying they wouldn't slip down stream. The river had grown wide and angry, full of trees and debris racing down to the ocean. The gravel and remaining asphalt on the road turned the area into a dangerous series of rapids, and even the slightest deviation from the path could cause the tires to lose traction and the vehicle to slip.

She'd become used it to a degree—just hold on tight—but when they reached the third river crossing, icy fear settled in her stomach. Here the water flowed at a frightening speed, a wrecked truck rested in a bush downstream, and there were heavy rapids right in the center of where the road crossed.

Her driver got out and poked around for a few minutes before settling on his chosen path. The SUV crawled across the river, the water slamming into the door midway up the frame and leaking in, soaking her boots and lower legs. He'd gotten stuck on a big rock halfway across, and needed to rock the SUV back and forth in the river a dozen times before gunning the throttle and pushing over the top, causing massive amounts of water to shoot into the vehicle.

Another thirty minutes up a steep gravel road and they finally reached Matapalo, and all Tasha saw was jungle in every direction. She hopped out of the SUV and walked over to a nearby shelter, waiving at the driver as he turned around and headed back to the town. Howler monkeys moved between the bamboo trees, calling to each other and dropping debris on the roof of the shelter. She checked her phone—no signal—so she pulled the tablet from its protective sleeve and looked at a saved satellite map of the area.

Beachfront houses and a smattering of eco lodges dotted the area. A couple of small streams ran through from a nearby mountain, dumping into the ocean in small deltas, and a single road ran further up the coast toward the national park.

"Two choices—beach or hillside," Tasha said to herself as she zoomed the map around. "Of course you can't see the houses through the damn jungle." She looked up at the imposing hill across the road, which had several seasonal waterfalls shooting down its side, courtesy of the rainfall.

She slid the tablet back in her bag, stood, and looked back up the hill, pulling her hood over her head.

"I hope he likes the beach better than the mountain view," she said as she turned and trudged through the mud to a battered wire fence. She examined it closely before reaching out and lightly touching the wire. Relieved that it wasn't electrified, she slipped over it and into the jungle beyond.

The rain had begun to stream heavily through the canopy, so she paused and put her backpack on under her raincoat, pulling the hood tighter around her hat and inching carefully through the trees.

Poison dart frogs hopped nervously away through the puddles as she approached the first house. It was a small structure, no screens on the windows and no AC unit that she could see. A man sat on the porch smoking a pipe and softly tapping his flip-flop on the deck in front of him.

She backed away from the house and worked her way further down the hill toward the beach, peering through her binoculars through the gaps in the trees. The heavy rain and her camouflaged raincoat gave her almost perfect cover. Twice she scared some chickens out of the bushes, sending them squawking into the next nearest shelter. Once, a family of coati scuttled past her and into the household trash.

Most of the houses were quiet, waiting for the dry season to be rented out again. A couple in the house closest to the main path through the jungle were arguing about what to do for the day, their voices muffled by the sounds of the rain in the jungle.

The crashing surf grew louder as she approached the last few houses on the edge of the beach. Wind chimes sounded softly in the breeze, and she paused at the edge of the jungle, looking down the beach. Here, at the edge of the ocean, the wind finally blew the humidity away and she took a deep, relieved breath. Dark, volcanic sand lay unbroken for hundreds of yards in each direction. In far distance, near an exposed reef, she could just make out a man sitting in a folding chair with an umbrella propped up behind him.

She pulled out her binoculars and tried to focus through the light mist of rain and surf spray. The build was right, but she couldn't make out his face. As she watched, another man walked out from the tree line, wearing a head-to-toe raincoat and a wide-brimmed hat. He trudged through the wet sand until he was standing next to the man in the chair. She watched them talk for several minutes, and the man in the rain jacket dropped a bag.

The man in the chair made repeated gestures toward the south coast of Panama, faintly visible on the horizon. The seated man his arm dismissively, and the rain-coated man trudged back toward the jungle. The man resumed staring out at the water, pausing to pull a bottle of beer out of the bag.

Tasha lowered the binoculars and thought hard for several minutes before carefully packing them away. She ripped down several broad-leafed branches from a neighboring tree, shaking them to knock the ants off, then jammed them into the ground, making a small shelter. She crouched behind it, pulling her pants down and taking a pee on the soggy ground.

She sighed contently as she relieved herself, swatting at the mosquitoes on her butt and legs. As she stood and started to pull her pants up, she heard voices close by—startlingly close. She froze. The rain picked up again, beating down on the leaf shelter as she tried desperately not to make any noise, ass hanging out in the breeze.

The moment she stopped swatting, the mosquitoes surged in on her, covering her in a thin film. She peered around the leaves to see a pair of surfers standing on the edge of the jungle looking out at the surf, barely six feet away from where she crouched. They chatted casually in Spanish, watching the waves and debating where the best path passed the reefs was.

Tasha bit her lip as the mosquitoes turned her exposed skin into a buffet, and ants began to climb her legs. She looked down, blowing softly at the bugs on her thighs and pant leg in a futile attempt to get them to go away.

Behind her, the two men started out across the sand. As soon as they got to the water line Tasha began vigorously slapping her bare skin and shaking her legs. Water that had pooled inside her pants while she was crouched poured down her legs as she stood up, stamping her feet to get the bugs out of her pants.

The more bugs she killed, the more appeared, until she realized in horror that most of the movement on the ground was not from the rain, but a swarm of insects trying to escape an onrushing horde of army ants. She snatched up her bag and sprinted into the jungle, bouncing noisily off wet plants and slipping in the mud until her arms and legs were covered in scratches and dirt.

She paused when she reached a small stream to check herself over. Aside from a few scrapes and a tear in her raincoat, she was mostly just filthy. Her bag weighed an extra ten pounds from the mud and water, and every inch of her itched.

"That'd better be him," she said in disgust, using a stick to poke around the edge of the stream for snakes. She crawled awkwardly down the bank, dropping into the cool water, letting it wash away as much of the mud as possible, and hoping to cool down after her sprint through the steamy jungle.

With renewed determination she crept down the streambed, using the stick to poke the banks and bushes for anything that might be lurking. She approached the beach again, paying much more attention to the ground as she slipped through the heavy foliage, looking for a landmark that would tell her how far she was from the man in the folding chair.

The man was still sitting on the beach, scanning the horizon through binoculars. From about twenty yards away, she could make out the trail of footprints left by the man in the raincoat. She followed them with her eyes till her gaze settled on a house nearly twice as large as all the others she'd seen further up the beach. It was elevated on stilts, with a deck wrapping around the beach side and a dark green metal roof. The man who had walked out to the beach was sitting on the porch, slouched in a chair and talking on a satellite phone. His body language suggested a mixture of boredom and annoyance, but of concern to her was the fact that he wasn't paying any attention to his surroundings.

She rose from her position on the ground and circled through the jungle toward the house, darting from one clump of vegetation to the next, the only sound the soft suction of her boots pulling free from the mud. Near the house, a group of birds fed from fruit in a hanging feeder, loudly calling to each other as they flew from tree to tree and back to the feeder again.

Tasha paused at the edge of the yard, scanning for any sign of people, then sprinted through the soggy grass to the north wall of the house. She crept toward the stairs, which appeared to lead to a side door that allowed access to a screened-in kitchen and dining area. She'd made it up four steps before she heard the porch creak, and the man who'd been on the phone called out, responding to a distant yell. He entered the screened-in area, cursed under his breath, and heard the phone beep as he plugged it into the charger.

Tasha dropped off the stairs and crawled on her hands and knees under the porch, sliding through the damp soil until she found the drain pipes coming down from the sink above. She hesitated before climbing behind the pipes, pushing thick spider webs out of the way and lying with her face down near the mud. She waited, easing her hood back so she could hear.

Heavy footsteps pounded up the stairs and strode angrily across the deck area, entering into the kitchen. .

"Did you get hold of them?" Knudsen's voice demanded.

Tasha could barely contain her excitement, her fist pumping slightly in the dim light. She cautiously slid her phone out of her pocket and held it close to her face, hand mostly covering the screen. Still no signal. She'd have to get to the satellite phone.

"Yes," the man replied patiently. "They said the road back to town is too flooded to send transportation and they don't want to risk trying to shuttle you off the beach because of the rocks."

"I'm paying them a great deal of money. The arrangement was that we'd meet them down here and they'd sneak me into Panama immediately. Not in two weeks."

"The DEA caught one of their boats, the back up boat isn't really made for getting in close to shore when the surf is this heavy. We need to wait until the rain clears to get back to town."

"It's the wet season. The rain isn't going to stop for two more months," Knudsen snapped at him.

"What do you want me to do? Call for a chopper? You said low profile exfiltration; this is low profile." The man's southern drawl emphasized the final syllable softly, his voice dropping to just above a whisper. "If Elliot hadn't gotten killed you wouldn't even be in this mess."

"Leave Elliot out of this," Knudsen said emotionally, "he died doing something for me, I won't have you blame him for your failures."

"He died at the hand of a lady cop who was still barely functioning from the last guy who beat her to a pulp. That's why I'm stuck in this goddamn jungle babysitting you."

"Babysitting? Listen…"

"No, you listen. They pulled me out of an op that was

paying triple my normal rate to come up here and help you figure out how to travel discretely to Venezuela. All you had to do was take the public bus and you'd have been through the border and into Panama no problem, smooth sailing from there. But you want private and you want expensive. So because somebody up my chain of command owed you a favor for God knows what, here I am trying to arrange a damn water taxi for you. Guess you're so helpless after all these years of servants wiping your ass that you can't do anything on your own!"

"There are dangerous men after me."

"There's a dangerous man in front of you." Tasha could see him lean in close to Knudsen through the cracks, staring intensely into his eyes. "Now, I'm going to hit the head, and when I come back, the phone oughta be charged and I'll try to reach out to somebody who can get you across the border. But if you can't find a way to control your temper, I'm going to renegotiate our terms. I think you'll find my negotiating skills are less polished than my superiors'. Are we clear?"

The boards near the center of the room creaked as Knudsen shifted his weight. He sighed deeply and answered. "Fine, as soon as the phone is charged you will get me a boat."

Tasha heard him the man chuckle under his breath as he turned and left the room, quietly shutting a door that led to one of the bedrooms, and leaving Knudsen alone in the room.

The sounds of Knudsen pacing near the kitchen counter echoed in the space under the deck before he stopped, leaning heavily against the kitchen counter above her head and staring out the screen toward the distant beach. Tasha watched through a gap between the counter and the tile as his breathing gradually slowed and his anger faded. He turned back toward the bar to make himself a drink and drank in silence, pondering the satellite phone.

Barely four feet below him, Tasha levered herself onto her

side and eased open her bag and took stock. She had a knife, six zip tie restraints, mace, a stun gun, a crescent wrench and a flathead screwdriver; not exactly the tools required to take on a mercenary and capture Knudsen. She inched her way back toward the stairs, stopping just under the edge of the porch and began to plan what to do.

Sneak outside, mace the merc through the bathroom window, or maybe stun him. Would have to be quiet. Restrain him and try to get an actual gun. Confront Knudsen, secure him, then use the satellite phone to reach Hopper. Hold them both in the house until Hopper can take custody, get Hopper to help out of the country.

Even in her head it sounded like a weak plan, heavily dependent on surprising and overpowering a paid mercenary quietly enough that Knudsen didn't take off into the jungle. She started to slip out of her raincoat when a noise above made her freeze.

"Son of a bitch, there's the boat now." Knudsen walked to the dining table and picked up his binoculars, then continued on toward the screen. "That asshole had them coming the whole time, he just wants more money," Knudsen said angrily, scanning the beach for people coming off the boat.

Tasha's heart sank; if there were more people coming, her odds were not looking good. She was tempted to rush the room, take Knudsen and drag him to into the jungle, but the thought of trying to negotiate the flooded river after even more rain had fallen sent chills up her back.

Tasha discretely slipped back to her hiding spot where she could see through the gap under the counter into the room. The door to the back bedroom opened with a loud creak and footsteps lead back into the room, water and sand dropping through cracks in the floor with each step.

"The boat is here! All that nonsense about them not being

able to land and here they are," Knudsen said triumphantly. There was a scuff on the floor as he turned to face the cooking area. "Now we'll both be rid of each other— Oh no. No, how did you find me?"

Tasha ducked down to avoid Knudsen seeing her. The footsteps continued steadily into the room, no hesitation. They paused several feet from where Knudsen was standing. Tasha stared up at the underside of the floor, heart pounding. She clutched her raincoat tightly, her nails piercing the fabric as the scene unfolded above her.

"Look, I know I didn't do exactly what you told me to do, I know I broke the rules. But I'm disappearing now; I'm going to a country they can't extradite me from. They won't even be allowed to question me. It will be fine. There's no need to be upset."

Tasha shifted position quietly, trying to get a look at the new arrival without success before settling for a view of Knudsen's head through a gap in the floorboards.

Knudsen's eyes flicked toward the bedroom the merc had gone into and shifted his weight nervously.

"Look, I haven't told anyone about our deal, not a soul. Nobody knows how you're connected to me, nobody even suspects."

"Elliot knew." Joe's unmistakable voice was calm and carried through the room. "Who else?"

"Elliot's dead! That man was loyal! He wouldn't tell anyone, he would never do anything that would endanger me." Knudsen's voice cracked.

"Sure he did. He indulged you. He indulged your habits and because of that, innocent women died. Those deaths attracted a lot of unwanted attention. The kind of attention that could link back to the medical treatment we provided you with."

"Lavoy said they didn't all die."

"Even a single death under such circumstances is unacceptable. You were specifically told multiple times not to risk contaminating them. The only saving grace is that you didn't sleep with a prostitute who might've spread it all over before realizing that she had it."

"A prostitute!" Knudsen's disgust overwhelmed his fear momentarily. "I would never."

"Prostitution is legal here. Did you have sex with anyone in Costa Rica? Anyone at all?"

Knudsen began shifting back and forth slightly on his feet, leaning toward the door leading out onto the porch. His eyes drifted as he searched for a way to avoid answering the question. Tasha was struck with the realization that the research student had probably contracted whatever Knudsen had. Her brow furrowed. What could he have that acted that so quickly on her, but had no apparent impact on him?

"I'll take your silence to mean yes. Who are they and where can we find them?"

Knudsen sighed heavily and tossed the binoculars on the table. "Playa Blanca, you can find her there. Student sea turtle researcher, she came here to do a monkey tour and their taxi broke down, so I entertained her. One thing led to another."

"Name?"

"Jenny something or other," Knudsen said.

"What's she look like?"

"Blond hair, dyed it looked like. From some town in Wales."

"Anyone else besides the guy in the bathroom helping you out here?"

Knudsen hesitated. "No."

"Don't mess with me. You can answer the question honestly or I can get my answers another way. But you will tell me the truth."

"My Helen's friend, Christopher. I told him I was coming down here to revisit the happy times from when Helen was younger and her mother was still with us. Told him he could go fishing while I stayed at the beach. He met Jenny and invited her over here. I guess he thought it would cheer me up to have somebody young around. There was a break in the weather so he took the truck into town two days ago to go out after sailfish, since then it has rained nonstop so the road is impassable. My plan was that when he was out fishing I'd travel to Panama and leave him a message saying I went to the doctor's. That he was to have fun and enjoy himself, and I would meet him back in the States."

"Last name?"

Outside, the steady rain slowed to a stop, only the water dripping onto the roof making noise.

"Weller, Christopher Weller."

"Anything else you need to tell me?

"No, I swear I didn't tell anyone anything. Look, you know I can offer you big money to help me get across the border. Once I get to Venezuela they won't be able to touch me. Then I will be gone for good, I have enough money..." Knudsen's voice trailed off and he let out a sob. "Look—"

Joe moved suddenly into Tasha's view, his hand flashing upward. There were two soft pops and Knudsen's body collapsed to the floor with a thud, shell casings scuttling across the floor directly over Tasha's head. She clenched the raincoat to her mouth tightly, covering much of her face, her eyes wide in the darkness. Blood began to seep through the cracks in the floor, puddling on the ground below.

A second man arrived from the direction of the bathroom, striding slowly across the room, the rustle of a large plastic bag in his hands filling the now silent space with noise.

"Bit of a bleeder," Lavoy's voice said.

"Side effect of the medication, blood thinner to increase the surface area of the treatment. Speeds up the effects."

"Well, well. Look who became an expert overnight."

"It was a long flight down. Let's get this mess cleaned up before some fisherman notices the boat."

Tasha slowly backed away from the growing puddle of blood looked back through the gap under the counter, watching them and trying not to make a sound.

Lavoy laid the body bag on the floor of the room while Joe wrapped towels around the remains of Knudsen's head. He poured quick-clot over the bullet holes and then tied the towels in a knot, putting pressure on the wounds. A small amount of blood seeped into the towel, but the mess was contained.

"Never thought of that."

"What's that?" Joe asked absentmindedly.

"Using clotting agent on a dead guy, usually I keep that around for when I get shot."

"Keeps the mess down. Less mess, less clean up."

"Agreed, I just never thought of it."

They grunted as they hoisted Knudsen's body into the bag and then slid the bag out of the way. Lavoy stripped off his latex gloves and threw them in the bag too, putting on new ones. He set his backpack down and pulled out some cleaner, handing Joe a bottle.

Tasha's mind raced as she tried to figure out what to do next. The thought of trying to sneak up on Joe was terrifying; doing it when Lavoy and possibly somebody else could spot her coming made it a nonstarter. The detective in her wanted to kick down the door and confront them, but the human with a healthy fear of death knew that doing so was foolish.

As they scrubbed the floor above her, she decided that her best course of action was to get to Hopper and send the DEA or

Coast Guard after their boat. Having settled on this, she crept away from where the men were working.

"Dr. K says we spray this enzyme stuff on the porous surfaces and it'll destroy the RNA proteins and kill the virus."

"Yeah, this isn't my first cleanup for him," Joe said. "I also found that putting sugar on the area afterward attracts ants, they strip whatever's left to nothing."

"Um, the ants can't become carriers can they?"

Joe stopped scrubbing and thought on it. "Maybe we'll skip the ants today."

Lavoy laughed and she could hear him spritzing enzyme on the spots. He leaned in close to the boards and shone a light down through the gap, dangerously close to where Tasha's foot had been just moments before.

"Looks like some leaked through, we'll have to get the dirt under the crawl space too."

"Alright, let's get the bag sealed up and I'll get down there."

Tasha felt a panic rush over her. She skirted the foundation quickly, heading toward the front of the house, looking back repeatedly to see if she'd been spotted. Joe and Lavoy finished with the body and Joe was halfway down the stairs when it dawned on Tasha that she should have gotten a sample of the blood. Not now. He was too close and it was too dangerous.

Without a second's hesitation she left the crawlspace and raced up the gravel of the driveway as fast as she could, cutting into the jungle and dodging clumps of brush as she tried to put as much distance between herself and the house as possible.

Joe stepped under the porch and stopped, looking down at Tasha's tracks in the mud. He pulled his gun and used a light to illuminate the crawl space, taking in the torn cobwebs, and the imprint of her body in the mud. He hesitated on the blood staining the dirt, looking at the proximity to a nearly perfect imprint of a female body. He followed the tracks around the foundation, stepping lightly, weapon at the ready.

The rain picked up again, and small rivers of water and mud flowed across the jungle floor. Joe stepped out from under the front of the house and stared up the driveway thoughtfully. He held that pose for a minute, watching the recent footprints in the mud form puddles. Joe's eyes tightened and he ducked back under the deck, out of sight.

CHAPTER FOURTEEN

Tasha sprinted through the mud, any attempt at stealth abandoned as she vaulted up the staircase of the house she'd seen the college couple staying in and burst through the door. They were enthusiastically making love on the bed, the girl clenching the mosquito net in pleasure with her back to the front door. Tasha raced through the house, dumping the girl's purse and a couple of bags until keys to one of the dirt bikes outside clattered to the floor.

She snatched them up and ran through the bedroom, leaping out the open window and running to the parked bikes, the girl's startled yelp following her as she ran.

She pulled the plastic rain guard away and tried to jam the key in the first bike's ignition. It went about halfway in before getting stuck, and she yanked at it, knocking the bike over in her haste. She looked back over her shoulder at the wall of jungle plants behind her and tried the next bike. The key inserted cleanly and she jumped on, standing up to violently kick-start the bike.

It roared to life, and she clenched the brake and hit the gas, spinning it around on its front wheel and sending a stream of mud and gravel against the side of the house. She let go of the brake and the bike leaped forward, nearly unseating her as she lurched up the driveway toward the main road.

She thought back to the map. The road leading to the national park stopped at Carate and the only other direction to try was back through the freshly swollen rivers toward town. She climbed the hill back to the main road, bouncing up the uneven gravel.

She reached the road, careening to the right toward Puerto Jiménez, accelerating as hard as she could without losing control in the surface water. She chanced a look over her shoulder, checking for signs of pursuit but finding none.

The bike rumbled to a stop at the edge of the river. Several feet of water now covered the area the cab driver had crossed earlier, and there was fresh wreckage just off the road—a small hatchback had been washed away. She scanned upstream for shallower waters.

Several trees had tipped over up river, diverting the water and causing it to spread out over a large area. A goat meandered across the river, up to its belly in water, and Tasha knew she had found her way across.

She gritted her teeth and swung the bike around, fighting her way up the edge of the swollen river to where the goat was standing. It scampered away in terror as the dirt bike's engine screamed through the water. Tasha looked downstream and revved the engine, pushing out into the river flow.

Water slammed into her, driving the bike off course, but she leaned into it, putting her leg out for balance as she revved the engine and steam poured off the muffler. Halfway across, a large piece of teak tree rushed past, its branches crashing into her thighs and leaves whipping her face. She cried out in pain and gunned the engine again, using the tree to help her gain traction across the river and up the bank on the other side.

She accelerated the bike, back on the road in one piece, and raced toward town, laughing into the wind as the adrenalin took hold.

Joe made one final pass through the house, checking for any remaining evidence of Knudsen's stay, then stepped off the porch. Lavoy was just finishing loading the second body bag into the back of the small ATV they'd appropriated, and he turned around.

"Too bad we had to clip him."

"Boss said no witnesses," Joe grunted back.

"Even so, he's just a bag man."

"Nah, I checked him out before we got here. He's been working with a kidnap and ransom operation down in Ecuador. Those guys can't be trusted."

Lavoy shrugged, hopped in the driver's seat and turned the ATV on. Joe climbed in next to him, eyes fixed on the jungle as they headed toward the beach.

"Find any clues as to who it might have been?"

"I think I know. I've seen those boot tracks before," Joe said softly, his eyes scanning slowly in every direction, submachine gun across his lap ready for use.

"Former coworker?"

"That detective. Strauss."

"Down here? That seems implausible."

"I called in on the sat phone, she hasn't been at work for a while. They're checking her credit cards and phone records now. But I'm almost certain."

"Did you call our man at the harbor?"

"Yes, I told him to observe but not to act."

Lavoy looked sideways at him as the ATV rolled from muddy jungle soil onto the firm beach sand.

Joe sensed Lavoy's curiosity. "If she's smart, she's already phoned home. If she vanishes it gives strength to her story, even posthumously. If he just watches, her story can be discredited. Especially if we work fast."

"You mean Playa Blanca?"

"Yes. I'm starting to think the boss and I are very much alike. He had me make a deal with that aid group in Finca Limon on the slim possibility that Knudsen was both here and had slept with somebody. He valued operational discretion and mission success over money."

"Yeah, that's one of the reasons I came to work for the KSI, they have their priorities straight," Lavoy said.

"His forethought, our fortune. That contingency buys us room to maneuver without too much risk of detection. That's all you can ask for in a boss."

Lavoy slowed to a stop next to the boat, hopping out and dragging the first body out of the ATV while Joe grabbed the other. They heaved the two body bags into the bow of the boat.

"Come on, it's sixty-five miles to the rendezvous with the float plane. I'd like to get there in time to fish a bit," Lavoy said with a laugh before he put the ATV in gear and sent it rolling solo into the surf, its engine sputtering as the water seeped in.

Tasha had driven through the night to reach Playa Blanca, stopping once to get gas. She cruised the small town, looking for signs leading to the turtle conservatory without much luck. Eventually the long day without food got the best of her, and she stopped at a small soda.

Slumping into a plastic chair, she dropped her bag on the

ground and looked glumly at the menu. A young couple nearby glanced curiously at her torn clothes and the spattered mud across her body. The man hesitated, then leaned over and talked above the music. "Are you alright? You look like you had a rough day."

She nodded dully, still staring at the menu until it occurred to her that they might have the answer she needed.

"Do you happen to know where the turtle research center is?"

"Yeah, we work there." the man said with a broad smile. "You're a little late to participate in today's survey, but if you come by tomorrow you can join in. It's about fifty US dollars. You'll get to help us set safe capture nets and then bring the turtles in to measure them and take samples. We get as many as six turtles a day, although lately it's been around three. Green turtles mostly right now. You interested?"

"Not exactly. I met a girl not long ago named Jenny, and I wanted to get in touch with her before I left to head back to the States," Tasha said.

The man stared at Tasha disbelievingly. "Well, I'm afraid you're out of luck. She got some kind of jungle disease and had to be evacuated the other day. How long ago did you say you met her?" the man asked, leaning back slightly.

"About a week ago, in Puerto Jiménez."

"You got lucky, I think she went into the jungle after that."

"They just got her out, too. It was terrible. They said her kidneys and liver were failing. They checked her for all of the expected viruses and all but she came up negative. She was real lucky that aid agency came and got her, or else I don't think she would have made it," the woman added.

"Aid agency?

"Yes, a bunch of real pleasant fellows. They actually just left a few hours ago on their way back to a critical care facility in..." He looked over at his companion for verification. "Columbia right?"

"I thought it was Panama, but whatever. Saved her at the last moment."

"You guys don't seem too upset," Tasha said curiously.

The couple looked at each other, and the guy shrugged his shoulders before the woman leaned over.

"I don't know the circumstances you met her under, but between the two of us, she wasn't exactly, you know... A good girl."

"What do you mean?"

"You know," the woman said uncomfortably. "She was always starting trouble. Mostly over men or drugs. I think she'd slept with about half the researchers."

"Not me, I know better," the man said with a smile, squeezing the woman's hand.

She smiled back at him and continued. "Anyway, there's no telling what she got into. They said it was some kind of virus, but it could have been a bad drug reaction. They were going to kick her out of the program a month or so back, but for *some* reason they let her stay."

"Did she sleep with anyone else after she got back... recently?"

The girl shot Tasha a piercing stare and then laughed. "Why? Are you jealous?"

Tasha did her best to appear hurt by the comment, and the woman continued.

"She was going to hook up with Benny, our Australian researcher. They were on the beach and he said it was all smooth sailing, but she started puking blood. So, I guess that didn't work out for him."

"Or did it?" Her male companion said with a chuckle.

The waitress appeared and dropped off their food, ending

the conversation. Tasha picked something off the menu at random and resumed her slouched posture, feeling defeated.

With Knudsen dead and his body in Joe's possession, and the sick girl having vanished, Tasha's only remaining hope had been to find Hopper in time to send him after Joe. She'd searched in vain for two days before admitting she'd been beaten.

Now she sat in the tiny airport in Puerto Jiménez, waiting for a flight back up to San Jose and from there to San Diego. Her clothes were worn and dirty, her spirit broken. To be so close only to have her suspect taken in front of her had set off a spiral of "what if" questions in her mind.

What if she'd moved in on him earlier? Just gone for Knudsen as soon as his bodyguard left the room?

What if she'd confronted Joe and Lavoy when their guard was down? Could she have stunned Joe before he could react?

What was she going to tell Jackson when she got back home? That she'd found Knudsen but hid in the shadows while he was murdered in front of her? Should she tell him at all?

A plane made a smooth landing on the runway, and she gathered up her belongings, her plastic boarding pass clutched in her hands. The plane didn't have the normal colorful markings of the local airline, and she squinted at it as it taxied down the runway towards them. A short, fat man in an airline uniform spotted her confusion and interjected with a friendly smile. "That's a private charter, miss. Your plane'll be here in twenty more minutes."

"Thanks." She set her bags down again, deciding to get some more coffee from the nearby table.

A man bumped into her, apologizing as she was knocked off balance. She reached up and inadvertently grabbed his shoulder in an effort to right herself. When she straightened, her eyes shifted from the ground to his face, and she froze, gaping at the steel gray eyes staring down at her. The realization hit them simultaneously, and she took an inadvertent step back.

"Hopper! I've been looking everywhere for you," she said, still clutching his shoulder.

A few people in the small waiting area glanced up from their morning coffees, but their interest soon waned.

"Really? I wasn't aware you were here, Detective. Seems like this isn't your jurisdiction?"

"I need to talk to you," Tasha said in a low voice, glancing at the other men standing near him. "I have some very important information about our suspect and I need your help to—" She trailed, then reached out and felt his jacket between her thumb and forefinger. She met his eyes. "Nice jacket."

"I'm actually retired from the FBI, down here on a bit of vacation. The private sector does have some perks," he said, straightening the jacket out.

"Retired," she said slowly. As she took a step backwards she noted he wasn't alone; a pair of tall Americans with beards and loud shirts stood nearby watching her curiously. "Seems like you found a way to leverage your previous position to your advantage."

"Indeed. Now if you don't mind, our flight is here."

He brushed past her on the way to the door, pausing and turning to say one last thing.

"Strauss? Sometimes losing is winning in the end. If I were you, I'd be careful about how you play the game from now on. These players have a long memory."

He gave her a slight smile and headed out to the private plane, leaving her gaping after him.

CHAPTER FIFTEEN

Tasha walked into her apartment, tossing her keys in a bowl and stripping her clothes off as she wandered into the living room. She tossed her khakis and blouse in a pile on one end of the couch and pulled on a pair of sweats that she'd snagged off the table. She dug around in the pile of clothes and pulled her badge and gun out, laying them on the table, then leaned back into the couch and turned on the TV.

She'd decided to tell Jackson what happened—all of it—and he'd sat there in silence, not writing a single note. At the end he looked emotional and turned his computer off. They sat there in silence for a good five minutes before he finally spoke.

"Take a week off, paid. Then back to work. I want you to know I appreciate all you've done. So long as I have this office, I will cover for you. But I want you to know this—we lost this one. There's no going back and trying again. It's over."

"Over," she mumbled to herself. "Over."

She flipped through the news channels, pausing at the scene of the latest murder near the causeway to see if she knew any of the people processing the scene, then continued until she found the weather channel. Nothing but clear skies for the rest of the week, no sign of rain any time soon.

Thinking of rain brought back a rush of memories—the constant wetness, the humid air on her face, those empty beaches. Knudsen's blood slowly dripping through the cracks in the deck to puddle in the soil below.

"It's over for Knudsen anyway," she said to the empty room.

After she'd left Jackson's office, two FBI agents had stopped to talk to her. They'd finished processing the files from Knudsen's house and wanted any last notes she had. They freely shared what they had, and she showed them all her reports from the massive forensics study they'd conducted on the house. They didn't seem surprised, just interested in closing the case down and moving on. On a whim, she'd asked if they knew Sullivan or Hopper. The lead agent had given her a curious look and told her that he'd heard they'd both retired.

After that the conversation stuck mostly to chitchat, until nearly the end when they were packing up to leave. The lead agent turned to her and thanked her for her help, and then offhandedly asked her a question.

"How was your vacation to Costa Rica?"

She froze, unsure what to say, but he continued packing up, evidently unaware of her reaction. She steeled herself and feigned innocence.

"How'd you know I went to Costa Rica?"

"We've been trying to get your reports for two weeks. It's rare for a lead detective to leave right in the middle of a case that connects a murder, a massive bush fire, and a missing person. They said the stress of it all combined with that reporter hounding you and your recovery from the previous case led to you needing time off, that's all. Was it a good trip? I've heard it's very pretty down there."

"It rained every day, but when it cleared up it was beautiful," she said, as cheerfully as she could muster.

He searched her face for a moment before smiling and shrugging it off. "My wife is always talking about going to see the whales and turtles down there, I might send you an email asking for recommendations for sightseeing some time," he said putting the last hard drive into his bag. "Well, we'll need to get going. Thanks for all your help, Detective. We'll let you know if Knudsen or any of his men turn up. Have a good one."

If Knudsen turned up. If they only knew...

She stared at the TV, her right hand idly twirling the drawstrings of her sweatpants and her foot tapping her badge where it rested on the table. Night slowly overtook the valley. Streetlights flickered to life, and the flow of traffic ebbed as people settled down for dinner.

Her thoughts were interrupted when the lights, TV, and her phone all abruptly lost power. She sat up in the dark and felt around the table for her weapon, drawing it from its holster and slowly standing. With quick steps she moved to the corner of the room, using muscle memory to avoid tripping in the process. She crouched in the darkness, waiting.

The TV came to life again, showing a wall of static. She lowered her weapon and took a deep breath, smiling into the dim glow from the TV, chiding herself for being so jumpy. She took a step back toward the couch and stopped in her tracks, eyes fixed on the TV.

A series of images almost buried in the static flashed past—ballistics reports on the bullet that had killed Helen, an internal audit chiding Tasha for poor detective work and her lack of investigative paperwork, an internal memo requesting clarification on which cases she was working, crime scene photos from the hospital, post-fight pictures from the kidnapper's ranch and the hospital detailing her injuries, pictures of the dead and missing from the investigation, and a final picture of Knudsen arriving at a beach resort without a care in the world. The final image froze on the screen for a long minute before fading away, replaced with another image of Knudsen dead on a metal table, two bullet holes in his head.

A sound broke the static, wavering as though the signal wasn't quite strong enough. She stepped closer, listening intently as a disembodied voice spoke.

"This journey is over, it's time to move on to other things. Goodbye, Detective. Good show."

The TV abruptly turned off again, plunging the room into near total darkness. Tasha stood stock still in her sweatpants and bra, trying to discern the telltale sounds of somebody else in her apartment, her suddenly sweaty hands gripping her gun. Time crawled while she waited to see if Joe would arrive to finish her off. Suddenly the power was restored to her apartment, the cable box coming back online and the lights flaring bright.

She shielded her eyes in surprise and swept the room, looking for any sign he was still lurking in the shadows. Breathing heavily, she swept the apartment room by room, checking every corner and every closet, under the bed, in the air conditioner closet. After about a half-hour she was satisfied he wasn't there, and she sat down heavily at the kitchen table, pouring herself a glass of wine.

Staring into the glass she made a decision. She knew the risks and she knew the odds, but it was the only path she could take.

"Better run Joe, the law is coming."

EPILOGUE

"All things considered, it could have gone better. We've cleaned up most of the loose ends. I wouldn't say it was pretty, and it certainly attracted a lot of unwanted attention, but it would seem that the investigations have run their course and we're in good shape." Lavoy finished his briefing and sat down.

Ed Stokes sat next to Joe with his hands steepled together. He looked up without moving his head. "Most of the loose ends? You mean with the exception of our wayward detective."

"Correct. She still has enough intel that she's... proving to be problematic."

"Good choice of words. She seems to know enough about Kapple and Green that they've both picked up federal chaperones. Also, we were audited by National Institute of Health. They were asking about unpermitted medical research, and they have been camped out on our networks trying to break our crypto ever since she talked."

"In our defense sir," Lavoy broke in, "they've been trying to get through our crypto wall for a while now. This just got more of them on it."

"So... the detective?" Stokes asked.

Joe's lips twitched. "I've had many opportunities to resolve that problem. I've chosen not to."

"Why?"

"Honestly?"

"Yes."

"I felt by this point that she had been discredited enough with the public that she posed little direct risk to our activities. If she had turned up dead, it was possible it could have attracted renewed interest in the case."

"That's a large risk to take, not just for you, but all of our programs. Is the difference she makes worth it?"

Joe leaned forward on his forearms and looked Stokes in the eyes.

"A government structure still following the basic rule of law enables us to be effective. If anarchy rules, it's hard to plan for all possible contingencies. The death of a police detective would have had unpredictable outcomes, potentially making far worse problems for us than what she can manage on her own. Sometimes, destroying something isn't the right approach. Isn't that what you told me on my first day?"

Stokes sat back and smiled, thinking back to the day he'd first met Joe. "Yes, that's what I said. Although I didn't think it would cause me this kind of headache." He gazed at the ceiling in thought for a minute before continuing. "We're moving Dr. Kapple to the Moon Based Training Center. His research, too. I'm going to have Steve accompany him and blend into one of the construction crews heading out to the new base around Saturn. The FBI is all over you right now, Joe, and your former agency is digging as well. We need to stash you until this calms down and they stop looking. Hatfield is prepping to take over Saturn construction in about two years. I'm going to need you to hook up with him and act as a bodyguard and enforcer. We can't afford Saturn to revolt or be stolen by another group, it's key to our long-term strategy. You've worked with Hatfield before and he respects you, so this is a natural fit. Concerns?"

Joe was silent for a long time, staring hard at the floor before shaking his head no. Stokes looked to Lavoy who shook his head as well and the two subordinates stood up to leave. As Joe reached the door, Stokes asked him one last question.

"Any regrets?"

"Never. Life is just experiences wrapped in poor choices. You can't have one without the other. Besides, sounds like I get to see another planet."

Stokes smiled and Joe left the office, followed by Lavoy. Stokes wandered over to the whiteboard in the corner and reached for his phone.

"Dana, bring Green and Hatfield in here. We need to talk about the future of the KaliSun Initiative."

THANK YOU

Thank you for reading *Going Viral*. If you enjoyed it, please take a moment to leave a review on Amazon, Barnes and Noble, Goodreads, or your preferred online retailer.

Reviews are the best way to show your support for an author and to help new readers discover their books

Milton Keynes UK
Ingram Content Group UK Ltd.
UKHW040659050124
435493UK00001B/77